The Twelve
Days of
Christmas

Love
Among Us

The Twelve
Days of
Christmas

Stories by

C.C. CARGNONI

Book Cover Design by The Book Cover Whisperer:
OpenBookDesign.biz

Tools and apps:
www.Wikipedia.org
www.fotosketcher.com

Library of Congress Control Number: 2021922936

978-0-578-30188-4 Paperback

FIRST EDITION

CONTENTS

Preface

May peace come upon your home.

With many strugles in our lives, we sometimes forget the feeling of wonder that a newborn baby brings.

The Christmas season can be bitter-sweet. Hectic gift purchasing, tension between friends and family, and demands from our workplace, among other issues, can take the joy out of the season.

Restore the joy. Stories share emotions and create memories. By having tradition and storytelling during the Christmas season, joy transcends time to be relived over and over again, in our memories and our hearts. Share your story.

Each year I place ornaments with pictures of my family upon my Christmas tree and say an individual blessing for each one of them for so many wonderful memories. My mission is to relate the sisterly and brotherly love of the Christmas season.

To focus on how we are blessed, despite worldly dynamics and distractions, is the essence of hope. I hope that the stories herein will bring peace to the reader in this fast-paced modern world. I encourage everyone to share their Christmas memories with their families. My effort in relaying the stories is a dedication to all the angels in my life that herald God's presence.

Follow the tradition of reading on Christmas Eve to enjoy this book for a Christmas celebration. Or with one story for each of the twelve days of Christmas, take time and reflect on the joy in life. Love is present during the Christmas season. May the reader carry the wonder of birth and creation from Christmas into the New Year.

*"We are all meant to bring God
into the world for God is always
needing to be born."*

Meister Eckhart (Modified)

Love
Among Us

The Twelve
Days of
Christmas

Introduction

A grain of truth shines through in each story; the truth of God's love, the truth of miracles, and the truth about our humanity. The twelve days of Christmas provide a period to reflect and rejoice. The season promotes generosity and love.

The first story, *A Gift of the Heart*, found inspiration through the song originally known as the Carol of the Drum. The popular Christmas song, written by the American classical music composer and teacher Katherine-Kennicott Davis, is now known as the Little Drummer Boy.[1] As the lyrics layout, the boy only had his passion, his music to give to the Christ child. Lyrics: *I have no gift to bring pa-rum pum pum pum. That's fit to give our King.* Now the twist, perhaps that boy stayed in Jesus' life. Perhaps, what he witnessed was so remarkable that he was driven to dedicate his life to this child.

The next story *Away in a Manger* brings forward a bit of history of the lovely nativity set most of us display.[2] We envision being there on the night that Christ was born. We all become upset when the way we want to celebrate is disrupted. A little disruption can bring a whole new perspective.

Papa Panov's Special Day, originally written by Rubens Saillens and adapted by the renowned Russian writer Leo Tolstoy inspired *The Face of God*.[3] The essence of the original tale is given new life as the character, Opa Elder, is a shoemaker that lives a stone's throw from the town where Martin Luther posted the 95 theses of the protestant revolution. Opa is a little troubled between tradition and what Luther has posted. The new dimension of the story concerns peace within yourself.

A Victorian Christmas takes us back to London in a story inspired by the Little Match Stick Girl by Hans Christian Andersen. The original version emphasized societal inhumane behavior to a child in need. Christmas usually brings out the good in all of us. The story is rewritten featuring the determination of the little girl to realize her grandmother's dream for her. She has value. She has a purpose. Someone needs her as much as her needs are required to be met.

A Visit from Saint Nicholas addresses the

controversy that Henry Livingston Jr., not Clement Clarke Moore, wrote the poem known as *'Twas the Night before Christmas*. Although some experts are behind Livingston, various indications exist that Moore was the author as outlined in the story. Clarke Moore was a family man devoted to his wife and children. He was also a member of the New York Historical Society where Washington Irving attended. Although Livingston's descendants claim the poem as his, Livingston himself never claimed to be the author. Whereas, Moore did eventually claim it.[4]

The Best Gift, based on a true story, brings the reader to the twentieth century. The 19th century ended with a US Supreme Court ruling of Plessey vs Ferguson. The ruling stated people of color were separate but equal in the eyes of the law. A long time passed before people of color were legally integrated in the 1950s with the white population. Unfortunately, a certain amount of people still tried, in subversive ways, to keep blacks and other people of color out of neighborhoods in the 1960s and beyond.

Safe Haven produces wonder in a stormy night occurrence, a little eerie, like Dickens's, *A Christmas*

Carol. Also based upon a true story, the main character suffers from emotions that are evoked during the Christmas holidays when you have lost a loved one.

Based upon a true story continues as love continues to grow in *A Family for Christmas.* The inspiration came from a newspaper article about a family who discovered a half-brother existed while going through their mother's estate. A mother's love never dies. One wonders why the mother did not disclose the existence of another family member during her lifetime. The story takes up the theme and addresses an alternate scenario.

Santa's Helpers is a story that most of us experience when we take a tag for a gift from a giving tree during the Christmas season. Giving trees are in churches, in stores, and even in beauty salons. The general public's generosity to give continues. The story illustrates one family who needs a little help and why. Reasons always exist when someone's name is submitted for a giving tree or to be adopted by another family. Without asking many questions, many of us give so that everyone has a wonderful and blessed Christmas, even in troubled times.

A Christmas Miracle is a personally based story of healing. Even after the hospital threatened to stop life support, God found a way to keep a young man alive until human intervention could bring him back to life.

Sadly, *A Pandemic Christmas* was felt by people all over the world as we separated to keep each other safe from the Covid 19 virus during the 2020 quarantine. Months after the initial outbreak, brave people went back to work to be of service to the community. Doctors, nurses, and healthcare providers continuously were called to service. Eventually, people who served in the restaurant industry, to keep people feed, were also vital to the celebration of Christmas in 2020. The story developed from tales of people who could not visit families during Christmas. They contrived ways to bring their families together, happy to see them with internet access or drive by their house to wave through the window.

The tradition of the *La Befana* brings us in a full circle to the twelfth day of Christmas. The Magi arrived from the East, bearing gifts, to find the one who would free the people. The old Christmas witch inspired the story of the slave in the Roman province of Judea when the census was being taken in Bethlehem. The search for the Christ child by La Befana on the Feast of the Three Kings, Epiphany, is celebrated in Italy. She is similar to Santa Claus in the United States. She reminds us that the wise still seek Him.[5]

If we stop our busy schedule, we can find acts of love and caring every day. Find the love that surrounds you. The days between the birth of Jesus on Christmas Day and the arrival of the Magi, Three Wise Men, on Epiphany can provide joy and reflection to set the tone for the entire year before you. Love is Among Us.

MOST OF US WILL HEAR the song, the Twelve Days of Christmas over the holiday season. The original song had origins in England during the 1700's as a memory game. Some Christians have updated the meaning of the song to reflect their faith.

On the first day of Christmas my true love gave to me:

A partridge in a pear tree

New gifts are added each day:

Day 2: Two turtle doves

Day 3: Three French hens

Day 4: Four calling birds

Day 5: Five gold rings

Day 6: Six geese a-laying

Day 7: Seven swans a-swimming

Day 8: Eight maids a-milking

Day 9: Nine ladies dancing

Day 10: Ten lords a-leaping

Day 11: Eleven pipers piping

Day 12: Twelve drummers drumming

Each year, the cost to supply all these gifts is calculated. But, the ultimate gift is to love and be loved, which is priceless. The gift of the heart is the ultimate gift, as you will find out in the first story.

Endnotes

1   Wikipedia Boughton, Harrison Charles (1977). "Katherine K. Davis: life and work". Ann Arbor, Michigan: Thesis, University of Missouri, reprint by University Microfilms.

2   Thank you to the Conversation for information on St. Francis. -https://theconversation.com/how-st-francis-created-the-nativity-scene-with-a-miraculous-event-in-1223-124742

3   https://clausnet.com/articles/literature/papa-panovs-special-christmas-r50/

4   https://en.wikipedia.org/wiki/A_Visit_from _St._Nicholas

5   https://www.vox.com/21796404/12-days-of-christmas-explained

Day 1: The Gift of the Heart

"And you, O tower of the flock, the strong hold of the daughter of Zion, to you shall it come, even the first dominion; the kingdom shall come"

- Micah 4:8

JACOB HAD WITNESSED the night sky thousands of times in his young life as a shepherd boy. This night was special. He had never seen the wonder of the light from the star that blazed over Bethlehem like this evening. The light had started in the early evening. It lit up the sky and penetrated the cloud layer with wondrous colors, red, orange, and bluish purple haze. It could have been a rainbow if it were not expanded across the entirety. It mesmerized him. Each night, the shepherds told stories of God and His works while they watched the sheep and the evening sky. But this night, Jacob could think of nothing else than the absolute beauty of the light. He had been watching sheep for his Uncle Samuel since he was five years old when his parents had died of an unknown illness. His uncle had taught him the skills of being a shepherd. He watched over the flock of sheep at night with an older cousin, Jeremiah. Jeremiah was the first son of his Uncle's third wife. Since he was not to inherit his father's property, he and Jacob were assigned night time duty to watch over the sheep.

Living outside of the town of Bethlehem, by The Tower of the Flock which was known as Migdal Eder, was the only life he remembered. The shepherds of

Migdal Elder practiced the highly regarded trade of a proud Hebrew tradition. As a helper, he felt honored that he was part of the process that provided young lambs for sacrifice at the temple in nearby Jerusalem.

Jacob did not have much. He was privileged to be taken in and have enough to eat along with his humble tunic that provided for his clothing. His earlier memories of life with his parents blurred as stories told to him. Training to be a shepherd gave him purpose as it reflected the same occupation of Abraham, Moses, and King David.

He never tired of the story of King David. As just a youth, David was anointed by Samuel to be king. The story, like many others, was retold again and again, passed from father to son, of God and His covenant with humankind. Jeremiah's favorite story from the Torah was the telling of David's battle against the Philistine, Goliath. Jacob concentrated more on the idea of David's rich soul that resulted in psalms of love and praise to God. He loved the spiritual side of King David, not only the warrior. He imagined David leading the Ark of the Covenant into Zion, leaping and dancing with joy, playing an instrument, perhaps a flute. He imagined himself in the same manner but only he would be carrying his drum. His drum gave him a unique way to praise God.

Jacob had carved the drum himself during the many nights of watching over the sheep. He built different hollow carvings that made various sounds when he tapped on them. It was an extraordinary drum with tones. He always kept it with him.

He looked again at the light shining from the brightest star that he had ever seen. Jacob shouted out to Jeremiah. "Cousin, what do you make of this brightness that lights the sky?"

But before Jeremiah could respond, they heard a sound. Two strangers approached. Against the dust of the land, they dressed in pure white from head to toe. As a response, Jeremiah shouted to Jacob, 'Go retrieve my father to greet our guests."

As Samuel, the elder shepherd, approached the strangers cautiously. He saw that they had an entourage behind them. Samuel walked out to greet them. 'What might this humble servant do for you?

The first stranger responded in a resounding blast: "Do not be afraid. I bring you good news that will cause great joy for all the people."

Stunned, the shepherds fell to their knees. "Arise," the stranger spoke again.

"Today in Bethlehem, the town of David, a Savior has been born to you. He is the Messiah, the Lord. This will be a sign to you: You will find a baby wrapped in cloths and lying in a manger. On earth peace to those on whom his favor rests." Luke 2:11-19

Samuel hurried to gather a gift of the finest cloth in his house and take his favored son with him to Bethlehem to do as the strangers had said.

He turned to the boys, "You and you", he pointed back to Jeremiah and Jacob, "Get the finest lamb of our flock and carry it with you."

Jacob positioned the lamb's body on Jeremiah's upper back with its legs wrapped around his neck and shoulders. Jeremiah easily carried the lamb. Jacob carried blankets. Then he saw his drum and took it also.

The shepherds proceeded into Bethlehem as instructed. They went from door to door until they found where the newborn baby boy laid, in a manger surrounded by animals.

His uncle was doubtful but proceeded to present his gifts and pay homage.

Since the lamb needed to be attended, Jacob was instructed to stay behind when his uncle left.

Jacob settled himself with a blanket in the corner and awoke in the middle of the night to see the beautiful young mother cooing to her child. They seemed to be glowing ever so softly. The blue linen veil covered her head and fell softly over her shoulders, protecting both her and the child she held.

The baby gurgled. The mother, a young woman a bit older than Jeremiah, saw Jacob watching and waved him to come forward.

Jacob started to play his drum softly, tinkle, rap, rap, he drummed softly, like a heartbeat. The mother started to hum a lullaby.

He finished the light pattern that he had put the lambs to sleep with so many times.

"Music is my life and passion. I only have the gift of the heart to give to the child", mumbled Jacob when he saw that the child was once more sleeping. Mary smiled at him, "It is all God wants of you, love."

"How do you know?" Jacob questioned.

Mary's eyes danced, "I am the handmaid of the Lord. I spent many days in the temple, weaving veils and learning the word of God as a young girl.

I have received wondrous messages which I ponder and believe. God who is mighty has done great things for me. Holy is His name." The Magnificat.

A silent peace fell over the manger. The animals, all calm, made not a sound. Jacob found the peace comforting. He once again fell asleep in the hay, close to the mother and child. On the other side of the stable, Mary's husband Joseph regarded the boy. He appeared to be an impoverish child that could use a real home. He wondered if the boy's name, Jacob, was another sign from the Lord, as his own father had carried the name Jacob.

He looked at the carved drum and saw a real potential for this boy to work with wood. In the morning, he addressed the boy.

"Jacob, I have had a dream to take my wife, Mary, and the child, Yeshua, into Egypt. I will not return to Nazareth directly. Son, I have a very important job for you, if you are willing. I would like for you to go to Nazareth, to my carpenter shop, and seek my brother. I will give you my walking staff to show my brother the intent of my message. I would like for you to assist him in his work and keep my place until I return. He will honor the symbol. Our family are carpenters and he will teach you until I return."

Looking into the older man's eyes, Jacob desperately wanted to be helpful, but felt bound to the life that was given to him. "But what of my Uncle Samuel? I cannot repay his kindness with abandonment."

The elderly craftsman smiled at the boy. "If you are agreeable, I will speak with your uncle. I am sure it can be arranged. You can see that it will be many years before Yeshua will be working as a carpenter. I have considered that it will be helpful for him to have an older brother to support him when I cannot. You can also see that I am an elder."

Slowly, tears ran down Jacob's face, 'Yes, sir. I will learn to be a carpenter. Perhaps you will allow me to share my knowledge with Yeshua of how to be a good shepherd." He replied as he looked upon the beautiful child. Joseph's eyes crinkled at the edges as he smiled, "Of course, Yeshua will need to know much."

Jacob made himself as useful as possible to help the young mother and child over the next few days. Joseph sent to Migdal Elder for Samuel to negotiate the care of the boy. But Samuel refused to receive money in compensation for what he had provided for Jacob. "He has done the work given to him. You will find him faithful. If this is what the boy wants, he has my blessing."

Jeremiah hugged Jacob. "I will miss you, cousin. I will miss our evenings together."

"I will miss you also, but this is something I need to do for the woman and child. The man has asked that I help them. Many strange occurrences happened in the last several days. Wise men from the East visited to bring the child gifts. They dressed as kings. I overheard them say that the child was in danger from King Herod. Jeremiah, if I can help them, I need to leave you and all that I know here for a new life, for them. I know that the work of providing the sacrificial lambs is important. But this, Jeremiah, this is just as important, I can feel it." Jacob fervently responded

He hugged his Uncle Samuel in thanks.

"As the decision is done. Then let us be off," said Joseph as he tenderly placed Mary, with the baby in her arms, on the donkey for the journey to Egypt.

Mary called to Jacob, giving him her hand as she looked down from the donkey.

"We thank you for your kindness and help. I look forward to seeing you upon our return...." Her voice trailed off as she turned her head and looked ahead of her. The reports had reached them of Herod's slaughter of all males born under two years old. Mary considered her uncertain future. She and Joseph walked solely in faith as they journeyed to Egypt.

Jacob watched as they left until they were out of sight. His lower lip protruded with determination. Although frightened of the unknown life ahead of him, with Joseph's staff, Jacob turned in the opposite direction. He joined traveling companions to Nazareth as Joseph had arranged.

Jacob carried his drum by his side. With his soft sounds of his drum, he had given his heartbeat to the child, Yeshua. He would be the best big brother that any boy could ever want, he thought.

He didn't know it then but with his gift of the heart, he established what would become a long and loyal relationship between him, later known as James, and his brother, Jesus of Nazareth.

Day 2:
Away in a Manger

"Go rebuild My church, which is falling down."
– San Damiano Crucifix

"Dear God, dear God, you will never guess what that crazy *holy* man is up to now!" Anna woman cried out. The old woman came through the door of their family home with her hands together in prayer and raised them up to the heavens.

Anna attended morning services every day at 6 AM and lead her group in Rosary prayer. She considered herself faithful. She unwrapped the long scarf that served as the required head covering worn for church, displaying her gray streaked black hair. She proceeded to vocalize her dismay.

"Mama, mama, calm down. What is wrong?" asked her son.

"He's making a mess in the town square outside of the Church of the Virgen at the top of the hill. Of all times! He has animals and straw. We all had to walk around it after mass. The animal dung smells to high heaven." Anna proclaimed.

"Who? What are you talking about?" asked her son again

"You know, the crazy holy man. The one who stripped naked in the town square and said he didn't want anything from his merchant father, especially money. The crazy one that talks to nature and walks with the animals. The one that goes out every day and gives poor people the clothes off his back. Then returns to the monastery in rags. I've seen him and complained, but the other friars say they can't do anything with him. They all have taken a vow of poverty. That *one!* "

Anna's grandson, Giacomo laughed. "Nonna, he's not crazy. You think he is because he gives away all his money. But he believes that God will provide for him every day. There is no need to have anything when you go to sleep at night because tomorrow is a new day. He says his poverty is liberating. He never worries about the next day. Each and every day, God will provide."

Not satisfied with the answer, she huffed. "The friars take care of him, right? They put a roof over his head. They make sure he has clean clothes every day. When he stripped naked to renounce the greed of his father, the bishop came forward and covered him with his cloak. You would think he would be grateful. He forgets that I knew him when he was young and wandered the streets late at night. Just because being a knight didn't work out for him, doesn't mean he has the right to tell other people how to pray. He used to dress up fancy to go drink wine and carouse with friends, spending his father's money like it was water." She retorted.

"He is grateful, Nonna. He is. He is grateful for everything people give him, which is why he continues to pass it on to others. I know you are upset about what he is doing. But he is honest in his prayers. He sings to the sun and the moon. Nature and Francesco bond together. God touched his soul, like no other, and changed him." Giacomo felt he needed to defend the man who was so kind that all forms of animals gravitated to him. *The animals seemed to understand Francesco better than the town people,* he thought.

"Humpf!" replied Anna. She loved her ten year

old grandson but could not let him get away with impudence. She motioned as if to softly hit her grandson with the side of her hand on the back of his head. "Don't talk back to your Nonna, I am your grandmother. And don't get any crazy ideas, either."

Giacomo laughed again. The motion fell short in the air as he dodged out of the way, not touching him. It was more a symbolic gesture to give her respect due to a grandparent. He understood why she was upset. Her story rose his curiosity. He wanted to go see what Francesco was doing. His father saw the gleam in his eyes.

"Giacomo, do your chores, then you are free to go out." His Father knew him too well.

The chores took most of the morning. First, he fed the chickens and hunted the eggs. The chickens ran free so hunting took a long time. Then he delivered what fresh eggs he found to his father's customers.

As soon as he finished sweeping, he headed to the pinnacle of their little town. He saw the spectacle his grandmother described just as she had related it. In the middle of the square was a stable. Francesco had placed a cow, horse, and sheep around a feeding trough in the middle. The people attending Christmas Eve service would need to pass the smelly animals and watch their step as they entered the church. Francesco had made a mess in front of the church dedicated to the Virgen Mary. Not only his grandmother but other townspeople who gathered were equally upset and many had gone to the monastery.

"We can't help it", the head friar stated. "He has permission from Pope Honorious III." The pope had little choice as Francesco had given a sermon which convinced almost everyone that the Spirit of God spoke through him.

The townspeople muttered and accepted the word of the Pope. They considered their lot in life to indulge Francesco in his *holiness*. They would not have foreseen how this same man would someday become a saint. But it didn't appear to make his activities this Christmas Eve day any easier for them to understand.

After Giacomo had reached the top of the hill, he paused, breathing a bit heavily. He recognized the friar, a frail man, silently and slowly building an altar. His brown, ragged robes covered with dirt from the work.

As a young boy being less tactful and a bit bolder

than an adult, he approached Francesco. "Excuse me, but can I ask what you are doing?"

Francesco stopped his work and addressed the boy, "I am bringing Christ back to Christmas." He stooped over and picked up straw to feed one of the cows from his hand. "God asked me to rebuild His church, and I am doing that."

"By putting animals in the middle of the square to block the entrance to the church? You have upset everyone." Giacomo said woefully, in almost a whine.

Francesco smiled wryly, almost enjoying the discomfort he was causing. "Yes, I have indeed. People get uneasy with new ideas. I recently returned from the Holy Land. I want to kindle devotion to the Christ child and bring people together." He replied while he continued to work. "The church is too small to hold everyone. You will have to return for midnight mass tonight to get your answer."

Giacomo was perplexed. He had hoped he could get some information from the man to calm his grandmother. But apparently Francesco wanted everyone to find out for themselves.

Late that night Giacomo and his family dressed in their best clothes to attend mass. Giacomo ran ahead to get a good view.

There in the square was a woman dressed with a long blue veil over her head. She knelt beside the trough. A man in ancient brown robes stood beside her and two boys attended the sheep.

It appeared to be Mary and Joseph with two shepherds. Francesco had recreated the night Jesus was born. But where was the baby Jesus? Giacomo looked around. The people stared and wondered what would come next. No one had gone into the church. The priest in his formal robes blocked the entrance as he stood in front of the open double door.

The church bells began to ring: bong, bong, bong, twelve times. On the twelfth strike, Francesco emerged from behind the priest carrying what looked like a bundle in his arms. Giacomo realized it was a doll in the form of a baby. He approached where the woman knelt beside the trough.

Holding the doll in swaddling cloth high for everyone to see, Francesco then brought it back to his chest. He bent his head down and kissed the doll gently as if it were a real child. The first reported miracle happened. The doll appeared to be crying real tears of joy. He placed it in the manger. The priest then came out of the church and started the mass, right there in the manger scene with the Nativity.

Giacomo had never seen anything like it. In a grand gesture of equality, the rich stood side by side with the poor. People came together to worship the infant king.

He now knew what Francesco meant. Francesco brought people together. The people were the church. Perhaps Francesco felt he truly had accomplished the request God had made of him, "rebuild My church" through the devotion of the birth of Christ.

For days afterwards, Giacomo heard stories surrounding the Nativity stable. People reported other miracles. They brought their animals to be healed by the hay. People also took hay home with them to protect themselves from diseases.

Year after year, people recreated the scene of the holy family at Jesus' birth, a nativity. The practice was widely implemented. Statues of all sizes replaced live people.

In 1223, Saint Francis of Assisi succeeded in his mission to bring people together to relive the mystical event of Christmas, to be in the manger with Mary, Jesus, and Joseph. Through the centuries, homes celebrating the arrival of Jesus commonly have a Nativity set. All share the common experience, honoring the birth of Christ through the Nativity.

Day 3:
The Face of God

"Go to the poor. You will find God."
- St. Vincent DePaul

Decorations graced the small German town where die Opa Elder, a respected shoemaker, lived. Local juniper evergreen branches adorned every house and shop window. The location was not far from Wittenberg where the monk, Martin Luther, had nailed 95 protestant theses to door of All Saints' Church in 1517. Opa Elder had lived in Wittenberg at that time, and decided that the religious rivalry was too much for him and his family. He liked the peaceful comfort of a small village. Arguing about faith troubled his heart.

He had trained his sons also to make shoes. As they had grown to adulthood, they moved to their own towns far away. Each town, and surrounding area, needed shoemakers. The children called him Opa, grandfather, because he was a kindly old man, full of generosity.

He took delight in the precision that he practiced his trade. Each shoe was made to fit the person who ordered the shoes. Opa Elder learnt over the years that there were several common sizes and might have a pair available for a traveler that came into his small shop.

Unfortunately, his wife had grown sick several years ago with a fever that the doctor could not break. She had died and passed to spirit.

Each Christmas he would attend church alone and felt something was missing from the service. He longed to be reassured, to somehow see the face of God. Once again, this Christmas Eve, Opa Elder found himself feeling the loneliness of a man with a distant family and no companion.

That evening, he looked out the window and saw an old man that put the flame to the tallow candles made from animal fat to light the street. The candles stood in a holder about every twelfth house or so. The street seemed to be a blazed with light. *Maybe he was waiting to see if one of them would go out,* Opa Elder mused.

Opa Elder opened the door. "Come in," he shouted.

The old man was visibly shaking and glad to get a little relief from the cold.

Opa Elder said to the man, "I don't think I have seen you before. Are you new in the town?"

"Yes", said the man. "I am passing through for those who need me."

"Have you worked at this job for long?" Opa Elder queried again.

"No", said the man. "And it is much colder than I thought it would be. Thank you for asking me in your home to warm by your fire."

Opa Elder handed him a cup of broth.

"Your coat doesn't seem to keep you warm. I have a coat that might fit you," said the generous Opa. He went to the closet and took out a coat that once belonged to one of his sons. This is almost new. Please take it."

The old man was pleased and put on the coat immediately.

"I was just going to read from the Bible about the first Christmas. I found the tradition of birth especially interesting, Jesus' forefathers started with Abraham. Have you read the Bible?"

"Yes", said the man," I am quite versed in the Bible."

"Tell me then, because I come from an area that is in conflict with protests against the Pope. What are your thoughts about Jesus this special night? Is he present?"

The man replied, "It is no chance that I have come here this evening Opa Elder. I know that you are well respected and a generous man in this community. It will not do for you to have a troubled heart. I say to you, before Christmas Day ends, you will see the face of the Son of God. Jesus will visit you tomorrow."

"Only if that were true, but how?" But it was as if Opa Elder was talking to thin air. The man was gone.

He went to the door to look out. Again, he was greeted with the extraordinary blaze of the tallow candles which should have extinguished by this point.

Opa Elder scratched his head in wonder. He went back to the Bible and read the first section of Matthew again. Our family roots, it holds us together. Opa Elder thought as he read through the genealogy once again. Then he read that an angel visited Joseph to tell him to take the child to Egypt.

An angel visited Joseph, the words danced in his head. Was the old man an angel? He said that Jesus would visit him on Christmas day. He needed to be prepared. But Jesus could come in any form. The old man did not say. Would it be an infant? Would it be the carpenter?

Or would he experience the greatness of God through his Son in an unexpected way. Whatever form, he was excited but doubtful until he looked out the window once again and the tallow candles still blazed.

The next morning, Christmas day, Opa Elder rose early to see the street sweeper working. The winds whipped around building and the snow fell heavily as Opa Elder looked out. He could not allow the man to freeze to death. He opened his door and asked the street sweeper to come in.

"Thank you, thank you," repeated the street sweeper. Opa Elder handed him a cup of coffee that he had just finished boiling.

Opa Elder noticed that although the man had a hat and glove, his shoes had thin soles. He was almost walking on the ice. "I couldn't help but notice that your shoes are not the best condition. I am a shoemaker. Perhaps I can be of help."

The street sweeper looked down, a little embarrassed. "Yes, when you are on your feet all the time, walking in all seasons, it takes a toll on your feet. I have not been able to afford a new pair of shoes. As it is, I am too old to be out in the snow like this, I am the one that everyone expects to provide for the mouths to feed. My son is sick and not able to work now. My grandchildren are hungry."

Opa Elder had an idea. The shoes that he kept for a random traveler would be perfect for the street sweeper. Then, he had a hesitant second thought, what if Jesus came and he needed the shoes as a gift for Him. The man looked so forlorn. *If Jesus needs shoes, I will give him my shoes* thought Opa Elder.

The man was grateful and thanked him over and over. He was more prepared when he went out again to finish his job. "I will pray for you," he said in parting.

Opa Elder put a kettle over the fire and started cooking his Christmas dinner of cabbage soup. He cut up three heads of cabbage and dumped it in the water. Then he unwrapped dried carrots that he buried at the end of summer. He chopped them up and the final touch with a little dried sausage that he had saved.

When he looked up again through the shop window, he saw a young girl struggling with a bundle in her arms, fighting to move against the snow. Again, Opa Elder opened his door. "Come in," he called.

The young girl came inside with what looked like a baby that was so still that the child could almost be dead. "He is very hungry and cried so hard that he is exhausted from the hunger." She broke down crying. "I was going to leave him at the church as I cannot take care of him."

Opa Elder put his arm around the young girl's slumped shoulder in a comforting and fatherly fashion as he stood at her side. "Nonsense, let's not be hasty. A child needs his mother, who looks like she also could use some nourishment."

Opa Elder took the child from her arms. He noticed the poor little thing had no shoes on and his feet were like ice cubes. *I will make him a pair of slippers* he thought. He wrapped the baby from head to toe warmly in a blanket. He put him in a box for a bed and placed it near, but not too close, to the fire. He put a little water on the child's lips and he gave the young woman a piece of bread with some water. "Soon he will await and will be hungry. You need to be prepared to feed him. Do you think you can do that if you drink enough water?" Opa Elder asked. The girl nodded. He went to his closet and took out a shawl that had belonged to his deceased wife. Carefully, he wrapped it around the young girl. "You can stay here as long as you like. My home is small, just two rooms in back of this shop, but it is large enough to provide privacy for you to feed your child. You and your child have a home on this Christmas Day. Once you are ready, you can go forward again, if you still wish to do so." He gave her a piece of cabbage from the soup. She clasped his hands and said, "God bless you for your kindness."

Oh my, thought Opa Elder, *I completely forgot that Jesus was supposed to come to visit today. Hopefully, I did not miss Him.*

He left the girl sleeping in a chair by the fire holding the child while he looked out the window again. He only saw boys cheerfully playing in the snow which brought a smile to his face.

The storm had past. Throughout the day, Opa Elder would open the door to those who were cold and give them a little of his cabbage soup as he still looked for God to appear. *If Jesus comes, I have plenty to feed Him.*

That night, when night fell and the streets were empty, he looked out again to see the old man lighting the candles once more.

"Sir, come in. I did not get a visit from Jesus today after all," Opa Elder said to the old man as disappointment set in.

"I beg to differ," the old man said in return. Then the old man appeared to grow in stature as one in front of the blaze of candles. "God is in every act of kindness you performed today. You have seen Him in every face. And He has looked with mercy on your loneliness with the blessing a child in your home."

"But it was *my* gift that I was able to be of help to others," Opa Elder protested.

"Exactly," said the angel. And then disappeared.

Opa Elder looked at the young girl sleeping in the chair. True, she could be like a daughter that he had never had. The baby cooed at him. He thought again of the genealogy of Jesus who was also adopted by a human family. Whether she stayed or left, at least she would be strong enough to provide for the child. He hoped she stayed. He smiled at the baby and let the new life grab his finger with his small hand.

When the child also fell asleep, Opa Elder sat in his big chair and took down his Bible again. He started to read from the book of Matthew. "For when I was hungry, you gave Me something to eat...I was a stranger and you invited Me in." Opa Elder's heart was at peace. No matter the manner in which you worship, the path of love leads to God, he concluded.

Indeed, he realized when he serves others, he sees the face of God not only on Christmas, but every day.

Day 4:
A Victorian Christmas

"I can do all things through Christ
who strengthens me."
- Philippians 4:13

How beautiful the large fir Christmas tree displayed. The little girl looked down at the match bundle in her arms dismayed. She raised her head again to look at the green branches that bore candles burning brightly. The red bulbs hung on the tree reflected the tiny flames. The festivity inside the restaurant brought no comfort to the shoeless little girl looking through the window. She shook from the freezing weather outside, looking in. She stood there in hopes of selling just a couple of matches before going home, hungry.

The winds whipped around the corner. The

threadbare coat she wore provided very little protection. She had worn her mother's slippers when she left her home in the morning. Sometime during the day, a large slipper fell from one foot while she ran to get out of the way of a horse drawn carriage. She lost the other to a mean boy who carried it away to cause her misery. He laughed at her dire predicament. Her feet were blue and numb. She remained shivering with her match sticks, too afraid to go home as she had not sold a single bundle that day. Her father would beat her if she came home with no money. No one seemed to notice her, or they avoided her and looked the other way.

Dirt stained her face, sadness consumed her body.

She decided to cuddle against the building and lit one match for herself. She could try again once warmer. She found a small alcove by the corner of the restaurant and lit a match close to her feet. The heat against the frost was painful. She winced a bit. Then the back door of the restaurant opened and the man threw out the garbage. Food, it was food discarded from the plates in the restaurant. She carefully maneuvered to the trash bin and reached in.

She grasped quickly without looking. The owner

had caught her before and thrashed her as an example to others to stay away from his restaurant. She was afraid of his strong fists striking her. He shouted as he beat her, "Stay away. The people who dine here do not want to see the likes of you." Her hunger overcame her fear. She dared and retrieved a small piece of bread and a dirty piece of chicken.

She crawled into an unlit, dirty corner. She gulped down the food. So cold, so cold, she felt faint. Something drew her to crawl back and look into the front window of the restaurant again. It was the frozen stance of another little girl, present but ignored. Sitting at the table, so close but separated by the thick glass. She looked like a princess with a fine silken magenta dress and a big bow in her golden hair. She didn't know why but she almost felt sorry for the girl in the restaurant. The little match stick girl crawled away again. Her hands were warm enough as her father made sure she would have gloves to carry the match sticks. She managed once more to light another match to get a little warmth for other parts of her body, and again, her feet. This time she saw her grandmother, who had died in the last year, urging her to find heaven.

She limped back and peered over the top of

the outside of the window for a longer time. It was worth the chance of getting another beating, she was so enthralled with the girl. The scene of the Christmas celebration looked like it came from a fairy tale that she once heard. The little girl seemed to beacon her with an index finger that moved to summon. *"Come here, come here." She is calling to me, she needs me,* she thought. The little match stick girl didn't dare. Instead, she spotted a carriage that appeared to belong to this rich family. She climbed up to the edge where the footman would stand. She took a chance that no footman was needed on Christmas. Finally the family came out and the carriage started to move, the little match stick girl hung on with her life.

After what seemed to be an excruciating period of time bouncing, the carriage stopped and she rolled to the ground. She guessed correctly as she could hear a little girl's voice. When the family saw the little heap of rags on the ground, the father came over to examine it.

"Oh papa please, it is hurt!" came a high pitched sound from the little princess girl. "It's a vagabond," her father said in a grisly tone.

"Please, papa, please papa, can I have her for

Christmas?" She recognized the little girl that she saw through the window.

"No," her father answered gruffly. Then he addressed the coachman, "Take her back to the area where she climbed on. She must know where she belongs."

Victoria, in her desperation to salvage her request, threw herself between the coachman and the heap that was the little match stick girl.

"NO!" screamed Victoria in an act of defiance. With a stoic heart she stood staring at her father, her eyes were cold and blank. "I have no one, no brothers, and no sisters, no one to play with. Mother is always feeling faint and you are always busy. I am always alone. I want to have a friend for Christmas. I won't let you take her."

The strange look on the girl's face made the coachman stop and look at Victoria's father for further instructions.

The formality of the situation required that the father stay adamant against it, but he was not heartless. He had seen Victoria have a temper tantrum before over small issues, but her action was not a temper tantrum but a call for help. He had noticed how lonely his daughter had been. He should have put her in boarding school a long time ago. Every time he tried, his wife objected stating that she needed someone she could trust to be with and care for her when he was away on business.

"Victoria, you don't know what you are asking. It's a person, not a pet. I am sure she has somewhere to be." The little heap on the ground did not reply. "Oh, papa. If she agrees, I want her to stay for holidays. I can give her one of my old dresses and Marmee can help her clean up." Victoria stance changed as she pleaded. The father approached and gently nudged the little heap of girl in front of him with his foot.

He responded, "Very well. She can stay in in the carriage house with the horses if she wants to do so, and if the groom doesn't mind. Don't touch her until she is clean. I don't want you to get infected."

He turned around to go into the house. Her mother, horrified, did not come near the scene. Victoria turned to the little girl on the ground. "I do hope you will stay." She could not fathom what the little match stick girl had already experienced just to be there with her.

Victoria bravely ran to her father and grabbed his hand. "A friend, thank you papa, thank you. It is the best Christmas present ever." Her father picked Victoria up in his arms and carried her through the front door of the house.

"Now remember she is a person who might have a family that will miss her." His tone of voice turned gentle. The thought ran through his mind that he would eliminate this little piece of pestilence that had made its way into his home. Of course, he knew the little match stick girl would have a better life with them then on the streets of the city. He shouldn't indulge Victoria, after all it was a little girl, not a doll. He was afraid that Victoria would get tired of her new friend. But if that happened, he would see to it that this strange bundle would be taken to an orphanage, if she had no parents.

The coachman called for the groom then approached the little match stick girl. "What do you say?" The little girl nodded, yes, and picked herself off the ground to walk into the back of the house with him. The groom went to get the housekeeper to start the task. The next day was Boxing Day, the holiday that the staff celebrated. All the household staff took turns in the kitchen to share the same bathwater. The most prominent of the staff took the first turn and then it continued to the least. The little match stick girl sat still in the corner until everyone had had their bath. Marmee had given her a small cup of broth to drink. It had warmed her down to her bleeding toes which were now bound with cloth. She would be the last one to bathe. Finally, with the child's permission, Marmee helped the girl strip of her clothing as she sunk into the dark, black water.

"My goodness, you are skin and bones," Marmee exclaimed uneasily. Marmee had practiced some midwifery. She noticed the child's bloated stomach and recognized that she suffered from malnutrition.

Marmee carefully looked in her hair for lice and washed her thoroughly with lye soap.

The little match stick girl was quite attractive with the grime of the city removed. Since she had lost her baby teeth late, she still had a full set of permanent teeth when she smiled. Marmee burned her raggedy, stained clothes. She was clothed with some undergarments and wrapped in a blanket. The groom returned to take her to the carriage house to sleep with straw as a bed. With an actual warm blanket drawn up over her head, even with the horses, she slept soundly. It was the best sleep the little match stick girl could ever remember. She dreamt of her grandmother. "Grandmother, am I in heaven?" she asked. Her grandmother smiled. She thanked her grandmother for giving her the courage to hang onto the carriage.

The next morning the little match stick girl crawled out of her blanket. She found clothing, a second-hand, deep green dress beside her, and put on. It was the most elegant thing that had ever touched her skin. She sat and waited, content. She drank a cup of warm milk also left for her with a piece of bread and butter. She was completely alone with the horses. Everyone else was gone. Finally, Victoria arrived and chattered at her.

"Let's play tea. Can you tell me your name? It doesn't matter, I will call you Rose after one of my favorite stories, Snow White and Rose Red. Papa says you will need to go home sometime. But until then, can we play?" The little match stick girl stared at her. A name, she thought she had one but she had forgotten. The little match stick girl smiled, finally. Rose, yes, Rose would be a wonderful name. She had a name.

"Do you speak, can you say something?" Victoria continued babbling incessantly.

"My name is Rose." The little match stick girl finally said very slowly so that Victoria could understand through her thick cockney accent. Victoria smiled at her.

"I knew it, I knew it," squealed Victoria

And Rose knew she was in heaven, with a friend who redeemed her. She didn't care if Victoria's had selfish reasons for her to be there. She was grateful for the gift of a new life for Christmas. Victoria needed a friend. That was her gift. Rose would be a loyal friend to her throughout their lives.

Each year, they would tell the tale of their first Christmas together.

Each year the tale grew more colorful with added details, some true, some more enhanced by the years.

Each year, the two opposites recounted the tale of coming together.

One poor in spirit and one poor in wealth, needing friendship.

Both in need of the nourishment that the hope of Christmas provided.

Day 5:
'Twas the Night Before Christmas

"Let the children come to Me."

\- Matthew 19:14

PROFESSOR CLEMENT CLARKE MOORE stomped his black snow boots outside the foyer as he entered his New York City home. He didn't mind the light snow, it was the heavy wet flakes that bothered him. He brushed the flakes from the shoulder of his black long wool coat. He took time to make himself presentable. He sat down on the bench in the foyer to remove the heavy boots and put on his house shoes. He gathered his thoughts from his sleigh ride home.

Annoyance embraced him when he had gone out, but he didn't let it get the best of him. He wished that people could get along. Earlier in the day his eldest daughter had come home in tears. She was so distraught that she upset the entire family. She had gotten caught in the middle of an argument. Another girl had taunted her as a heathen because of the way the Moore family celebrated Christmas. Out of his nine children, she always could look with at him with longing eyes. Poor child, she was so empathetic and was quite upset about the incident. "Tell me, Poppa, tell me the best way to honor the birth of Christ?" she stammered through her tears. As a professor of divinity and biblical learning, he had specific thoughts on the matter. But he wanted to think more about how to reply at a level she would understand.

He need some time to himself to weigh the issue. He decided that sweet treats would bring back smiles to everyone's faces. So he rode out in the snow to get some for his children that late afternoon and pondered his thoughts on the matter.

Confound it anyway. In the 1823 years after the birth of Jesus Christ you would think people could agree that joy and love should dominate the season. Why fight over the way that Christmas is celebrated?

Even his seminary students' debated when Christmas should be celebrated. The argument seemed futile. The Catholic religion celebrated mass on Christmas Day. Protestant church members, like his own family, celebrated the twelve days of Christmas. The debate continued each year of exactly when and how Christmas should be celebrated. After all, no one knew when Christ was born. The Catholic Church had established the date to coincide with the winter solstice. It was an easy way to bring the pagans to the Christian celebration of life. As a professor and biblical scholar at the General Theological Seminary, his overall answer on the best way to honor the birth of Christ was to spread the love of God.

His thoughts always ended up with the same conclusion, people were missing the point. They should enjoy the beauty of the meaning of everything that symbolized birth of a child. People should be joyful, thinking of the new beginning, experiencing brotherly love.

He began the ride annoyed. The silence of the sleigh ride and the pure white of the snow gave him the opportunity to resolve conflict of the two methods of celebration. He thought about how to portray the type of innocent joy that Jesus Christ preached. After all, He had said, "Let the children come to me." Jesus often encouraged his followers as children of God.

What brings children joy? He mused. Playfulness came to mind.

Playfulness, he mused. He remembered that several of his own children had gathered around the old, round, Dutch handyman that came last week to fix the wooden floor. The workman smiled so wide that you could even see it through the big bushy white beard that he sported. He interested the children in everything he did. He entertained them with the amazing way that he worked the tools when he fixed various items around the house, enjoying their company as much as they enjoyed being with him. He even made small wooden toys for them. The Dutch handyman, just by his friendliness exuberated the kind of joy that innocence brings. For all appearances, he seemed very happy with his life and worked to make life better for others. In all of his acquaintances, Clarke Moore could not think of a more giving and amicable man.

In fact, the handyman made the perfect model for Washington Irving's character described in *A History of New York*. At a recent Literary Society meeting, he and Mr. Irving spoke of Irving's vision of Saint Nicholas as an elf. The vision amused the professor at the time. An elf-like Saint Nicholas seemed to him as a character that children could enjoy. He immensely enjoyed speaking with Mr. Irving concerning Dutch culture and traditions of New York State. His own wife, Catharine, was pleased that he had taken an interest in her Dutch heritage.

His youngest of his children rushed to him as he entered the house. "Papa, Papa." The housekeeper, Hella, took his gray wool coat and hat. He also relinquished the package of treats from his hand to her as he leaned down to hug the little tots. He felt that unconditional love from children was the greatest pleasure a parent could have.

"Children, children, Christmas approaches. Who would like to hear about Saint Nicholas?" he said grinning at them. He looked at his upset daughter who was also approaching as she descended the stairs. He addressed her, "The actions of Saint Nicholas might be the answer to your question of how to best honor Jesus at Christmas. The answer is to honor Him by the joy of giving."

His daughter's spirit rose, "Oh Papa, I certainly would like to hear about St. Nicholas and what he looks like."

"Well, most people think of Saint Nicholas in a traditional sense. His image is usually depicted as the white-hair bearded old man giving food and treats to the children, in his priestly robes, when he was Bishop of Myra hundreds of years ago," he responded.

The family headed to the dining room to enjoy the treats. Their father continued, "So many miracles were attributed to him that he is often called the Wonderworker. In that role, he is patron of many kinds of occupations. But recently, I have been considering that perhaps only in his role as the patron of children, his spirit might be reflective of the joy that children bring, a happy old soul."

"Tell us more Papa," added the eldest son.

"I have a colleague at the Literary Society, a Mr. Washington Irving. He referred to St. Nicholas in his book, *A History of New York, as St. Nick. The image of St. Nick is* that of an elf riding over tops of trees, flying through the sky, in a wagon when he brings presents to girls and boys. Close your eyes and imagine him. What type of animal do you children think might pull the wagon, maybe mules, because it would be so heavy?"

"Oh Papa," responded his daughter with a giggle, "Don't be silly, it must be an animal from where St. Nick lives in the northland, maybe reindeer."

By that time, Professor Moore's wife, Catharine, joined them. She teasingly scolded her husband for providing the treats, but she saw beyond the biblical scholar, distinguished professor, and leader in his community. She saw the loving father who adored his children, a family man full of love.

That night, when she called him to bed, he was still settled comfortably in his study so very late.

"Come now, dear, can't it wait until tomorrow?" She already had wrapped her head with a large handkerchief to keep it warm as she always did in the winter.

"I want to finish my thoughts from the sleigh ride today," he replied. She retreated with her candle in hand to the bedroom.

After their delightful treat time, he wanted to reinforce the vision of the elf Saint Nicholas and provide a *gift of a special poem to his children this Christmas.*

He filled his ink well and then put his pen to paper:

AN ACCOUNT OF A VISIT FROM ST. NICHOLAS

Everyone is in bed, finally, the house is so quiet.

'Twas the night before Christmas, when all thro' the house,
Not a creature was stirring, not even a mouse;

Reflecting on the day's activities and the children's chatter

The stockings were hung by the chimney with care,
In hopes that St. Nicholas soon would be there;

Finally, we got them all into bed after their treat

The children were nestled all snug in their beds,
While visions of sugar plums danc'd in
their heads,
And Mama in her 'kerchief, and I in my cap,
Had just settled our brains for a long
winter's nap—

*If an elf like Saint Nicholas arrived, how would
that sound?*

When out on the lawn there arose such a clatter,
I sprung from the bed to see what was the matter,

I've used this type of language before, but it is effective

Away to the window I flew like a flash,
Tore open the shutters, and threw up the sash.
The moon on the breast of the new fallen snow,
Gave the luster of mid-day to objects below;
When, what to my wondering eyes
should appear,

*Now the vehicle must be a sleigh like my own, and I do like
my daughter's suggestion of reindeer, what a clever girl!*

But a miniature sleigh, and eight tiny rein-deer,
With a little old driver, so lively and quick,
I knew in a moment it must be St. Nick.
More rapid than eagles his coursers they came,

And he whistled, and shouted, and call'd
them by name:

*Perhaps keeping with the Dutch tradition I will use ap-
propriate names*

"Now! Dasher, now! Dancer, now! Prancer,
and Vixen,
"On! Comet, on! Cupid, on! Dunder and Blixem;
"To the top of the porch! to the top of the wall!
"Now dash away! dash away! dash away all!"

More simile here will bring the reader to the scene

As dry leaves before the wild hurricane fly,
When they meet with an obstacle, mount
to the sky;
So up to the house-top the coursers they flew,
With the sleigh full of Toys—and St. Nicholas too:
And then in a twinkling, I heard on the roof
The prancing and pawing of each little hoof.
As I drew in my head, and was turning around,
Down the chimney St. Nicholas came
with a bound:

*I will honor to Dutch tradition and Washington Irving
in describing St. Nick*

He was dress'd all in fur, from his head
to his foot,

And his clothes were all tarnish'd with
ashes and soot;
A bundle of toys was flung on his back,
And he look'd **like** a peddler just opening his pack:

*Perhaps I will use a description of the Dutch repairman
that the children liked so well.*

His eyes—how they twinkled! his dimples how merry,
His cheeks were like roses, his nose **like** a cherry;
His droll little mouth was drawn up **like** a bow,
And the beard of his chin was as white as the snow;

Ah yes, the pipe, was included by Irving also

The stump of a pipe he held tight in his teeth,
And the smoke it encircled his head
like a wreath.
He had a broad face, and a little round belly
That shook when he laugh'd, **like** a bowl
full of jelly:
He was chubby and plump, a right jolly old elf,
And I laugh'd when I saw him in spite of myself;
A wink of his eye and a twist of his head
Soon gave me to know I had nothing to dread.
He spoke not a word, but went straight
to his work,

And fill'd all the stockings; then turn'd
with a jirk,

Irving used this description too, readers should recognize it

And laying his finger aside of his nose
And giving a nod, up the chimney he rose.
He sprung to his sleigh, to his team gave
a whistle,
And away they all flew **like** the down of a thistle:

*As a man of God, I want everyone to have good-
ness and peace*

But I heard him exclaim, ere he drove
out of sight—
Happy Christmas to all, and to all a good night.

*After all, he is a Saint and we are celebrating gifts brought
to the world...*

Professor Moore read through his poem once
more. *Certainly captured the playfulness I sought*, he
thought. The repetitive use of simile especially
pleased him. Relating the description to everyday
identifiable things for people creates images in their
minds. He thought using the word, "like", helped
to take the reader to the very night. As he thought
of the influence of the Dutch heritage, he knew it
would please his wife too. *I must thank Mr. Irving for*

sharing his knowledge. I am sure that Catharine and the children will enjoy this frivolous little poem.

The book, History of the State of New York, helped me describe St. Nick in the poem for my children, he thought as he concluded, and went to bed.

In the morning, the Professor studiously made some changes to the original version. When completely satisfied, he copied the poem several times as gifts to his oldest children. When Hella, his housekeeper came to the study, he read it for her. She laughed and asked for a copy for her children also. As he considered her as part of the family, he could not say no. Professor Moore provided one of the hand written copies of the poem to her. Considered such a trivial a piece of work, he did not bother to mention to her that it was a private poem. She enjoyed it so much she sent it to a local newspaper anonymously. She thought it too good not to share with all the children in future generations.

Clement Clarke Moore's was a bit surprised to open The Troy Sentinel newspaper two days before Christmas to see his poem, A Visit from Saint Nicholas, in print for all the world to see. Thankfully, no one knew he had written it. After all, he came from what might be considered an American aristocratic family. His father, Benjamin Moore, was of spiritual service to Alexander Hamilton. This type of tomfoolery was not tolerated in acceptable scholarly circles. Professor Clement Clarke Moore dared not claim to have written the poem until over 20 years after publication. Eventually, in 1846 when he published his book of poems, he included it. By that time, the significance of the poem outweighed what he thought was a frivolous scribbling.

He finally acknowledged the treasure he created as the general public recognized jolly old St. Nick, later Santa Claus, as our vision of joy and playful love in honor of the birth of the Christ child. After all, no matter our age, we all are children of God.

Day 6:
The Best Christmas Gift

"It's better to give than to receive"
- Acts 20:35

On the first day of kindergarten, Katie clung to her mother's dress afraid to move. Five year old children ran around in circles chasing each other. The mothers chatted with delight about the activity of the new school year. In a 1960 small community, most of the children seemed to know at least one or two other children playing in the room. Katie knew no one else. Her family lived in the back section of a large house divided into two units, which her grandfather owned. The only other children she had ever played with were her cousins. Anxiety shook Katie as she looked around. All the children sported their Sunday best clothing. Girls wore bright colored dresses and patent leather shoes. Boys wore suit jackets and short pants. Katie was no exception. She wore a lovely gold tone dress with a "K" embroidered on the sash. Her godmother gave it to her as a special present for the first day of school.

Katie's small size made her very shy. Going to kindergarten with all these strangers was the last thing she wanted to do. Katie heard her mother's stern voice, "Go sit down and listen to the teacher." She almost growled as she ripped Katie's hand away.

Katie entered the chaos of the room as her mother turned and waved an abrupt goodbye. Noise filled the air from all directions as children screamed and shrilled. Katie glanced around the room for a safe place to put herself out of the way. She spotted a little girl with skin the color of milk chocolate. She was the only person of color that Katie had ever seen. Katie wanted to cry, she was afraid and thought that little girl must feel the same because of the way she sat.

Katie almost crawled to sit next to the girl who wore a dusty pink dress, with her arms hugging her rolled up knees in a corner. They didn't say anything to each other, but looked into each other's eyes, both understood. If they could get through the day and go home, they would survive this change to their lives.

The kindergarten teacher clapped her hands with a burst of noise and brought the room to order. Ears perked up. The children in the class listened to her soft voice. She issued instructions to move them to different areas of the room to perform tasks. Katie moved. Her mother would be angry if the teacher wrote a note that she had not cooperated. She built up the courage to sit at a chair and table. As she rose from the floor, the chocolate colored girl followed.

A few hours later, the teacher dismissed the class. Katie put on her jacket as it was cool in Western Pennsylvania that time of year. Her new friend followed her down the sidewalk. Katie stopped, she stopped. Katie walked, she walked. Katie turned around, and the other girl stood like a tattered statute. "Where ya going?" Katie asked quietly. "I'm a-walkin' hume," replied the other girl.

"My name's Katie, what's your name?"

"My ma calls me Chloe."

"Do you live this way?"

"Yes'm."

"Ok, we can walk together?" Chloe was hesitant

to walk by Katie's side but Katie's insisted that it would be hard to talk to her if she was behind. They got to the corner where Chloe said, "I gotta go down this road." The only thing that Katie saw down the road was an old rotten barn that appeared to be falling over.

"Is that where you live?" Katie asked confused.

"Yes'm, me an' my ma stay there. My pa is gone." Well, sometimes Katie wished her father was gone too as he caused her mother to cry so often. "That is OK, as long as your ma is OK." For the first time, Katie saw Chloe smile broadly. "My ma is the best. She works hard for us and at night, we read by the candlelight together."

"Don't youns have 'lictricity?" asked Katie.

"No miss, we make do with what we have," answered Chloe.

Each day after that, Katie and Chloe played together during the hours at school. Then they walked home from school at the end of the day. In the beginning, at snack time, Chloe sat quietly while others munched their treats. So Katie brought snacks for her and Chloe to share. Katie's mother grew a little suspicious. One day she exclaimed, "My goodness, you must have a tapeworm." Katie smiled. "Yes, Mama, I grow hungry playing." Her mother would put in a bit more carrots or celery. Chloe was her secret friend. Her parents didn't have any friends that were Chloe's color. Although her aunt had a statue of a black man dressed as a jockey in her front yard that held a light. Katie didn't know why.

By Christmas, the two five year olds were forever friends. Before the Christmas break, the class was making a huge paper Christmas tree on the wall. Katie and Chloe cut out red paper balls and giggled as they stuck them on the green paper Christmas tree with glue.

It was the last day of school before Christmas break. Everyone pranced around the classroom, excited for Santa Claus. Chloe said, "I got somethin' kinda special for ya." "What, what, what?" Katie wanted to know. "It's a special present for Christmas," teased Chloe.

On the walk home that day, Katie talked incessantly about all the things she had asked Santa Clause to bring her. "I want a Chatty Cathy, Mr. Potato Head, and a Barbie doll. My cousin has a Barbie dream house but I don't think Santa could bring that," rambled Katie as they walked. Chloe didn't talk too much as Katie chatted on merrily, she was waiting for the right time to give her the gift. Then, Katie stopped, "Oooh, what is my present?"

Chloe smiled as she opened her hand which held a metal pin of a tiny black genie attached by a chain to a magic lamp. The genie sported a red painted vest and ballooned pants, his turban was green. Both colors highlighted the black painted skin. The lamp bore gold paint.

"Wow, thank you." Katie had never seen anything like it before. She only had an ivory heart on a gold chain that her grandfather had given her. She gleefully accepted the gift. Neither of them knew how to put it on so she held it in her hand.

Chloe said, "Make a wish."

"It's too special. I'll have to think of something good," replied Katie. They both nodded in agreement. She thanked and hugged her friend. "I don't have anything for you today, but I do have a doll I can bring for you after Christmas. She's not brown, but she is ever so cute." Katie wanted to share a treasured toy in return.

Then, what had been a very happy moment turned sour. Tears started to form in Chloe's sad dark eyes. "Mama and me, we have to leave. We can't stay here anymore. Mama said people are taking away our home."

"Why?" questioned Katie.

All the smiles had hidden Chloe's unfortunate life, and now it was time to go. The tears flowed freely as Chloe started to cry. She turned and ran in the direction of the old dilapidated structure that Chloe had called home, the barn. Katie didn't understand it at all. How could people be so mean? She stood on the edge of the sidewalk and stared at her friend as Chloe ran away. Then she reached the old barn and disappeared from Katie's life.

Who would want to live in that broken down barn anyway, she said to herself with disgust. She turned toward her home and kicked the sidewalk again and again as she advanced toward her house. Why would Chloe leave her when they were such good friends? Why would Chloe give her something beautiful like the genie pin and then run away? This time when she went into her home, upset, Katie told her mother about Chloe and the pin. Her mother was angry, took the pin and threw it in the trash with unkind words spouting out. Katie cried. Her mother spanked her and sent her to her room. Confused by the hurt of losing her friend, and her mother's anger. Katie thought about the warning her mother gave her, "Don't you dare tell your father about that little girl."

Later that night, in the stillness of the dark, Katie listened to hear if her family was asleep. She slipped into the kitchen from her little bedroom that had been a closet. She searched through the trash and retrieved the pin. She hid it from her mother under the deepest part of the mattress. When she made her first wish on the genie and the lamp, she wished she could give Chloe a home for Christmas.

Not that dirty old barn, she wanted Chloe to have a real home.

Thirty five years later, Katherine sat at her desk reviewing the morning reports. When she looked up, she saw a co-worker, Robert, walking slowing toward her with his head sunk low. He looked like a defeated man. Katherine did not know Robert, as they were on different marketing teams. She had seen him in meetings now and again. Katherine was a little annoyed wondering what he could want. She needed to get the reports done so she could pick up her sons on time from school this afternoon.

As he approached, she greeted him. She couldn't avoid it. "Hey Robert, how's it going?" she asked. His red eyes watered as he spoke very low. "Not too well today," he mumbled. She continued to watch him as he was slow to begin speaking again.

"You see, I don't have anywhere else to turn, and someone on my team said you might be able to help."

Great, she thought. "Well, if it is one of the reports, I'm sorry, I am already scheduled to leave in a couple hours so I can't help you there."

"No," he responded.

"Ok, then, what can I do for you?" Katie queried with a light voice.

Again he reiterated, "I don't have anywhere else to turn. I have asked all my family, friends, and people I know, so you are my last hope."

"Oh, it can't be that bad," she replied smiling. "What is it that you need?"

He stood in silence for what seemed to be a long time before he replied. Finally, he said, "Money, I need $1,300.00 before tomorrow for a home I wanted to buy for my family." He added very quickly, "I am told that you might be able to help me out and I swear I would repay you."

The statement shocked Katherine. "Why would you need $1,300.00 by tomorrow? Didn't the bank give you a closing statement?" Katherine knew that this was odd. His dark eyes mirrored sincerity. He made direct contact with Katherine's eyes. "Yes, and I did have all the money to close. But, this morning the realtor telephoned me. The neighborhood association requires $1,300.00 deposit for the reserve account. Without the payment, they will not approve the sale."

Robert shook his head back and forth. "Where am I going to get $1,300.00 by tomorrow?" he whined, talking to himself aloud more that directing the statement at Katherine. "Wouldn't that be the seller's expense?" Katherine wanted to know. "The realtor said the seller refuses to pay it at this point and they have another buyer that will," he responded with confusion.

"I bet they do," she quipped. Then she decided on a practical approach, "About the money, did you talk to human resources to get an advance on your pay?"

"Yes," he groaned. "That is where I got the majority of the money for the closing costs. Believe me, I have pieced together the down payment from every source I have. I drained every resource. If I had anywhere else to get money, I would not be in front of you."

"Well, there will be other houses," Katherine spoke gently.

"But this one is perfect for my two children, I need this one." Robert emphasized.

Now, Katherine understood what had not been stated. He suspected that a sudden expense imposed was not in accordance to HUD disclosures requirements. He wanted a home, not a fight. If he reported the potential violation to HUD, it would take time. Besides, he would need to prove that the neighborhood association acted wrongfully. He needed help, not a legal battle to make a point. He wanted his children in a better school district this coming school year. Any legal battle he might start due to the violation of disclosure would take time. Time he did not have if he wanted the house for his family. The house would sell to someone else. Katie had an inkling of a thought of what might have occurred. The deposit had taken the form of a legal barrier of entry to stop his family from entering into the neighborhood because they were black. She wondered if the neighborhood association would have presented this sudden issue to a white family.

Still, $1,300.00 was a lot of money. Her current weekly grocery allowance was approximately

$45.00. If Robert didn't pay her back, she and her family would be eating pasta and beans for a very long time. She risked a poor Christmas celebration, without money for presents, if he defaulted. Lending him the money presented a great risk. She didn't know him, she worked with him. Yet, he looked sincere. Her blood boiled with the injustice to keep his children out of the neighborhood. She thought of her own three sons. She was lucky enough to have a home for them. His head hung low as he waited for her answer.

"How do you propose to repay?" she finally blurted out.

"I can make thirteen $100.00 payments, plus 10% interest, every payday," he responded desperately with a tad of hope in his voice. She looked again into his eyes to see if she could tell if he was being honest about this unexpected expense.

"No," she insisted. "If I lend you the money, I don't want interest. I only want my money back. Repayment along with mortgage payments will be a strain on you, how are you going to manage?" Katherine asked as she looked at him sidewise, still trying to grasp the circumstances of the sudden expense.

"My wife is going to start working part time, we can manage the payments," he reassured her.

A few more minutes of awkward silence passed. Her mind raced through of all the reasons she should not give him the money he needed. He now sat down, clasping his hands together, praying. The injustice of this surprise expense more than irritated her. She deemed it inequitable to rob this man and his family of their potential home.

Minutes passed in silence. He rose and started to pace nervously.

Cutting the tension she finally said, "Ok. I guess you need the money now to deposit in the bank today so you can write a check tomorrow, right?"

He stammered, he could not seem to get the words out, "Thank you.. you... you. Yes, I ...I need to deposit the money as soon as possible."

She grimaced and reached for a blank piece of paper. Scribbling out a promissory note, she instructed him to sign it and get two other co-workers to witness his signature.

Robert composed himself and took on the task with a renewed purpose. He was back in a half hour with the witnesses. Katherine gave him gave him a check. Then it was necessary for her to get to the bank and transfer the money from savings to checking. She telephoned the Director of Human Resources, who was already aware of Robert's desire to secure a home. The company management agreed that she could leave work immediately to get the funds transferred on her way to pick up her sons from school.

Robert honored his word. Pay dates were the 1st and 16th of every month. For the next 13 pay periods she found a check on her desk. They never discussed the transaction again. Upon receiving the final payment, she marked the promissory note, "Paid in Full." She handed to Robert. He shook her hand, then pulled her toward him in a slight hug. "Thank you so much," he said. "My wife is so happy. My kids started school and talk about it every night at dinner."

In late November of that year, Katherine decided to take another job and moved to a new location. She celebrated Christmas in a new home. After the New Year started, she received a Christmas card in the mail forwarded from her old address.

We can never thank you enough, we love our new home. Merry Christmas, Robert, Chloe, Robert Jr. and Jeannie.

She studied the picture of the smiling African American family on the Christmas card. "Chloe", she mused. "Chloe" The name sounded familiar, echoed in her mind, something from her past. She had not thought of her kindergarten friend for a long time. Over approximately ten years, she had hidden the genie and lamp pin in various places. One day, she came home from high school and the pin that she kept in the back of her personal effects drawer was gone. Her mother had found it and threw it away. Even then, her mother's bias prevailed. She looked at the Christmas card again. Could it be "*her*" Chloe? She had never even asked Robert about his family. Maybe it was "*her*" Chloe, maybe it wasn't. It didn't matter.

She smiled to herself, finally the first Christmas wish she ever made as a child on the genie finally did come true. She helped Chloe have a real home for Christmas.

Day 7:
Safe Haven

"Light shall shine out of darkness."
- 2 Corinthians 4:6

No one likes a Scrooge, Marie realized as she dreaded her plans for the day. If she were going to entertain this holiday season, she felt that she needed to decorate a bit. At least she would try to put on a brave face. She ran her right hand through her short gray hair, pushing it back out of her face. A scene outside the large living room picture window caught her attention. Her heart skipped a beat. She noticed her neighbor struggling to weave his Christmas lights in and out of the short bushes in front of his house. As in a trance, she stared at him for a long time. Last year, her husband Frederick, Freddy for short, had helped their neighbor position his Christmas lights. Freddy, being an engineer, organized his own decorations and then lent a hand to anyone else who needed it. Making the world sparkle by putting up lights during the Christmas season delighted Freddy. He often said the job combined a creative skill with his engineering ability. *Funny how you remember small ordinary events like that when you have lost someone,* she reminisced. Last year, she had carried two mugs of steaming hot chocolate with mini marsh mellows to them. They laughed over the eight foot Rudolf the Red-Nose-Reindeer in the adjoining yard.

She missed her husband who had died suddenly of a heart attack while gardening this past year. She found him lying on the floor, lifeless, in the kitchen when she had come home from work. Freddie was still dressed in his garden overalls. The event still churned in her mind from time to time.

With frantic trembling, she had telephoned 911. Maybe, just maybe he was still alive, although not moving. *Help, please help my husband,* she had desperately pleaded to the operator. She was still huddled over Freddy hugging him when the police officers arrived. A detective handed her a homicide investigation card. "We have to investigate even what seems to be a natural death", he had said. The words stung. The events of the day still made her wince as she remembered the nightmare. She knew that Freddy would not have wanted that for her.

She hated decorating for Christmas this year because it meant that she would be celebrating without him. Christmas would happen this year, and every year after, without holding his hand at church, without his warm smile over the special brunch prepared for friends, and without small thoughtful little gifts to unwrap.

No warmth, no love, no Freddy.

Freddy had always decorated with classic white light outlining the house and electric candlesticks in the windows. Marie was in the middle of placing the candlesticks in the windows when she spotted the neighbor. She knew if she asked, the neighbor would help her put up the outside lights, but she couldn't endure the pain of walking into an empty house with Freddy's lights greeting her.

She wanted to cry but felt like she was too spent to do so, as she wiped a small tear from her eye with the back of her left hand. Since his death, she worried whether Freddy had gotten enough satisfaction out of life. He was only 62 years old. He hadn't gotten the chance to ever enjoy life without getting up for work for a 9-5 job every day, except for vacation. He usually took one week vacation to play around in the garden. He called those his lazy days. Since Marie taught school, he took a second week vacation with her in the summer to travel. They had had more plans of traveling and growing old together. But that was not meant to be.

She continued to watch the neighbor struggle with the twinkle lights as she struggled with her own memories. Everything seemed so tangled.

After a while, a glow snapped Marie from her thoughts as she noticed the neighbor had plugged the lights in. She stepped back from the large window that let light and warmth flow into her home.

She looked up. A fresh swag of pine should adorn the large window as it had in the past. Freddy had loved the smell of pine this time of the year. She had forgotten to order it. Well, she thought, placement and plugging in the electric candlesticks would one of the sure things she would do this year. Freddy would want her to do at least that much without him. On their very first Christmas together, Freddy had explained that a light in the window always welcomed a weary traveler into a home. The light indicated that the home was a safe haven where the person could rest. His family carried the tradition from Ireland where a light placed in the window on Christmas Eve welcomed the weary, holy family traveling from Bethlehem. It was an old custom, which meant any visitor was welcome and the light acted as a guide. When he was a child, his family used real candles. Freddy loved the custom and bought an electrical plug in candle for every window in the front of the house, eight in all. She took the first candle in her hands and for a moment, looked at it, and held it against her chest near to her heart. Then she went from window to window, placing the candles, thinking of his many wonderful traits that made her fall in love with him. Her first thought centered on the way that he cared for her, always making her a cup of hot tea after a tiring day at school. She continued to place the candles as she thought of the fun they had together, how they laughed at crazy plays on words. Being an English teacher, his love of the use of language attracted her when they meet through her friend, a co-worker at school. The friend had brought her brother, Freddy, to the spring picnic. Everyone teased that it was love at first pun for Marie and Freddy. She chuckled at the memory as the pain of loss struck at the very center of her heart.

Then, of course, she had to face unwrapping the Nativity set that Freddy's mother had gifted them when they wed. The Nativity was another important tradition for Freddy. He liked to build a large wooden structure for the stable and put it at the foot of the fireplace. But Marie thought, this year, she would place the figures on the mantle as no wooden stable was available. Each statue, painted in beautiful colors, stood a full foot tall except for Mary. In a royal blue cloak, she knelt beside the baby, Jesus. With loving care, she placed the baby, the symbol of hope, peace, joy, and love, in the manger and covered him with a cloth. On Christmas day, she and Freddy would uncover him. But not this year.

Marie continued throughout the day, placing a Santa here and an angel there. With each placement, Marie started to exhale a small prayer under her breath for their love. She and Freddy had recently celebrated their 40th anniversary, without a major argument. Sure, they had their heated discussions, and some were real doozies. But, they adhered to the adage to never go to bed angry. So it bothered her a bit, as the day wore on, that her annoyance was growing toward Freddy. The same memories that evoked her love for him, caused her to miss him. She would never have her happy ever after in her retirement and old age. *How dare he not take care of himself,* the phrase stuck into her thoughts and repeated over and over. She should have insisted that he take regular medical exams, she reprimanded herself. *But he wasn't a child! A yearly checkup wouldn't have killed him! In fact it could have saved his life.*

Marie wrapped her small frame in a shawl as the darkness crept in and the day turned to night. The temperature become a bit colder. She sat down to a dinner of leftover hot homemade chicken noodle soup with a bit of salad. That evening her feelings of loneliness made her eyes swell up with tears. *He shouldn't have died, he should be here with me.* Anger rose to the point where she wanted to bang the table with her fist, but she felt beleaguered. She slumped involuntarily.

With no children of her own, emotions of isolation and hopelessness filled her. She and Freddy had seen a specialist when they had had trouble conceiving. The words etched into her brain, "So sorry, there is nothing that can be done." Freddy held her in his arms as she wept that day. With her head against his chest, he stroked her hair and comforted her, "You have your children at school. They depend on you. Look at the wonderful influence you are on them." The memory pushed the flood gate of emotion open, grief struck at the very core of her soul.

She and Freddy had talked about adopting a child. Ultimately, Marie's students were her children. She treasured the memories of her class room students. Yet, but sitting in the house now, all alone, did not put a telephone in her hand to reach out to one of them, as she might her own child. As the emotions flowed, she put her hands over her face, and continued to cry. When she finished sobbing, she looked around through bleary eyes. Then she took several minutes to calm down and gather her thoughts.

Marie felt weak but knew she would feel better if only she could do something purposeful. She cleared the table and washed the few dishes, leaving them to dry in the rack. *"I have to get my mind off of me and onto others, enough self-pity."* She had bought beautiful Christmas cards. Snow covered trees with white glitter filled the background. The foreground pictured a lion lying with a lamb. She bought it because it symbolized peace, so gentle, serene. This, she decided, would be the perfect evening to address them.

She approached the big wooden desk in the den and sat looking outward where she could see the lights in the front window. One card for her sister, one for her sister's children, and another for Freddy's brother. The snow started to fall and the wind was blowing a bit harder now.

The house, being a built around 1925, creaked with age. The lights began to flicker from the storm. *"What a horrible night to lose power."* Marie pulled the shawl still tighter around her. *I may need a flashlight, she thought.*

She rose to retrieve the one she kept in a cabinet above the refrigerator in the kitchen. Then, suddenly, a pitch darkness enveloped her. But not completely black. Illuminated in front of her stood the familiar figure of her husband. Almost in a whisper, his name escaped from her lips, *Freddy.* Marie rubbed her eyes in disbelief, she wasn't sleeping and she wasn't dreaming.

In the doorway, as big as life, was Freddy. He was dressed in his gardening clothes. His tall body appeared a bit transparent but she clearly saw the charm of his smile and the softness of his brown eyes as he gazed at her.

The several seconds that their eyes connected seemed like an eternity. The fear that had first seized her turned into a warm feeling of inner peace. Freddy turned and took two steps toward where the electric candle had lost its glow. Almost, in slow motion, he turned back to her. His right arm extended toward her, inviting her to take his hand, still smiling, still present, offering his comfort. She lifted herself from her chair ever so slowly, her knees felt weak. Trembling she reached out her right hand in response.

In a blink of an eye, he was gone, with only the flicking of the returning electrical light shining again. The power restored. His appearance hit her like a bolt of lightning as she dropped back into her seat.

Amazed but happy, a smile crept upon on her face. She knew that he was alright. All her anger from the day dissipated, all her thoughts of loneliness were gone, and so was her sadness. Her husband was okay, and smiling.

Marie sat and reflected for a very long time. She remain still, not moving too much in any direction in fear that what she felt would be lost. She considered the illogical event of what had occurred.

Finally, she placed her hands on the side of the chair and pushed up again. This time feeling a bit stronger. She stumbled a bit as her feet shuffled forward. Marie stood in the place where Freddy had stood. She tried to soak in the feeling of wonder of his being and the warmth of his gaze. She understood at last, that he was truly happy where the light had guided him to a safe haven. She felt close to him.

The spirit of love filled her. Something drew her to the Nativity, the eternal travelers of Bethlehem. She uncovered the baby, Jesus while she lovingly said under her breath, "Merry Christmas, Freddy." She could almost feel him with her.

This very night God revealed love and mercy so she felt it timely and symbolic to reveal the Christ Child. This is what God sent to the world with the birth of his Son.

United in God's love, she could put her worried heart to rest. She understood. More so, she knew that she could look forward to a time when she once again would be held in the safe haven of Freddy's arms.

Day 8:
A Family for Christmas

"For whoever does the will of my father in heaven is my brother and sister."

- Luke 8:19-20

YOUNG AND ALONE, Sophia wanted to provide a loving family for her baby boy more than anything else in the world. But she also knew she would not be part of it.

The nurse gently lifted her hand away. In a low and soft tone the nurse spoke to her, "It is time." Sophia nodded yes and released the baby, her heart tore in two. Logically, she knew this was the best course of action for both of them. A stable family would provide love and care in a way that she could not provide.

She used the small amount of insurance money that she received from Bill's accidental death for his funeral. Only a little over a thousand dollars remained to provide support for her and her son. He needed a solid foundation. She would be able to start a new life.

But, something that looked so right on paper felt so wrong within her, she still moved through the process. She made three conditions to what otherwise was a closed adoption. First that her son's name would remain William, after his father. The second, she would receive an unofficial a report about her son each year from the adoptive parents. Lastly, she insisted that they have financial means to send her son to college. The barren couple agreed to all conditions since they knew they would not be able to have children of their own.

Shortly after Sophia had celebrated her 18th birthday, she married Bill, her high school sweetheart. The couple went their against their parents' consent. Their families objected to a union of the couple with different ethnic backgrounds.

Her grandmother would say to her, "Marry your own kind, you will have enough other things to argue about." Her mother was softer in her approach and tried to reason with her. "Sophia, you are so young, so much of life to experience. If he loves you, he will wait for you." Her father expressed a stronger objection. "You do this, you are no longer my daughter." He had said. But, she was too much in love and too young to think that love would not solve every problem. They both believed that in time, everyone would approve. Time was not on their side.

Sure, they struggled with money as most young couples. Funds were always tight, but love and happiness filled their one room apartment. Their joy was complete when they had found that Sophia was to have their first child. Sophia worried, but Bill reassured her with a simple plan to build a family. Bill would work for a year while Sophia got her associate degree and then go to college while Sophia worked. He was certain that his sister would help with the child as she already had several of her own. Fate was unkind. Bill died in a tragic hit and run car accident a little over a year after the wedding. Her parents offered no support nor sympathy.

Sophia felt the guilt and blame of Bill's death from his parents. Although they came to the funeral, they made it clear they wanted nothing to do with her, or her child. The anger and hurt of losing their son overwhelmed any acceptance of a grandchild.

Bill's mother had caused a scene at the funeral home. "If he had gone to college, he never would have been killed by a car walking home from work so late at night." His mother had screamed at Sophia. Bill's sister hugged her mother and stayed to calm her as the funeral director escorted them out, turning away also. His father left in a bad temper.

Her parents did not come to Bill's funeral. Her hope that they would reconsider their relationship due to her pregnancy faded. Her father continued to forbid any member of the family, even extended family, to contact her. She was truly alone in the world.

She felt she had no choice but to offer the baby for adoption. The first year she found herself looking longingly at babies at grocery stores or even at the park. She carried one of the small crocheted squares with her, always. She grieved for at least two years and accepted the free counseling sessions offered at the adoption agency.

Life continued for Sophia. She worked her way through college as a waitress. Only traditional female jobs were available for women at the time. She did it for Bill. She knew that Bill would have wanted her to complete her education. He always encouraged her while other men she knew thought she would be lucky to take dictation. While she was earning her degree, she met and married a nice boy that she met at the university. Sophia lost her second husband to a heart attack that ended their 34 year marriage. She bore three daughters, but no other son.

Through the years she would remember her son's birthday. She knew exactly how old he was. As promised, the adoptive parents sent a yearly report, via the agency, which gave details of her son's progress. She managed to sneak to one of his baseball games when he was 10 years old. When he graduated law school, she cajoled an invitation to the ceremony from a secretary. She promised to support one his fellow foreign students who had one to attend in the audience. So the secretary agreed. After the ceremony, she almost went up to him to say "Hello." She stopped when she saw his adopted mother hug him. She felt she had made the right decision for her son, but her heart still ached from the loss.

Years passed. At 59 years old, as cancer began to consume her, she wanted closure. She now lived with her oldest daughter, Mary, and her son-in-law in their home so that they could care for her. Besides, she loved seeing her two grandchildren every day. As always, seeing the smile of a child brought joy to her heart.

Autumn trees exploded with color. Sophia watched the falling red, orange, and yellow leaves from her bedroom window. Trees showed the signs of change with upcoming winter. She observed it. Sophia knew it was time for her to share her secret. One evening Sophia called her daughter, Mary, to her side.

Lowly she whispered to her: "You have a brother" Mary was not sure she understood what her mother was trying to say to her.

Confused, she responded. "Yes, mama, I know, we are all brothers and sisters through our love of God."

Sophia managed a slight smile. She knew this revelation would shock her daughter, who was very faithful.

Sophia continued, "Sweetie, let me explain. I married before I met your dad. You have a biological brother." Mary stopped her actions in mid-air, thought her mother was rambling, than started to move again. When she looked at her mother's earnest face, she knew what she was stating was true. She dropped into a chair, stunned.

Sophia proceeded to tell her the story of the poor young woman, full of hope and love, whose life included a son. That son was her brother, Will. Mary could not believe what she was hearing. "Did daddy know?" more of a demand than a question. Sophia continued in a weak voice." Yes, I told him when we met and we never spoke of it again."

"Mama, what is it that you want me to do? Why are you telling me this?" Mary stammered.

"Mary, I would like you to contact your brother,

Will. I want to see him again and invite him for Thanksgiving dinner, give him a chance to know his biological family."

"I don't know, Mama," Mary said, almost in a whisper.

"Please, Mary, it is my dying wish," she didn't want to do it, but she pulled the guilt card. She was desperate to know and see her son.

"Mama, this isn't fair and you know it." Mary moaned.

"Please, Mary." Sophia repeated and pleaded with her eyes as well as her words. Mary's cold, stunned stance on the issue began to melt.

Mary knew she needed to approach this situation delicately. She knew how shaken she was with the news. She could only imagine Will's reaction. She felt that she no longer knew her mother. As much as she was shocked, she knew her siblings would be too. She shuddered to think of how she would handle it all. She realized that if she was to have peace after her mother passed, she needed to do this for her.

For the next few nights, Sophia would ask if Mary had contacted her brother. Each night Mary responded, "Tomorrow, mama. Give me some time to think this through." Her head hurt thinking about the upcoming encounter.

Several days afterwards, Mary reluctantly dialed the number to Will's office, a secretary that acted as a gatekeeper, took the message. She would learn more about Betty, his secretary, as the calls became more frequent.

Mary reported to Sophia nightly that there was no response. After ten days, Sophia pulled out the sentimental piece of the crocheted baby blanket that she had kept. "Here, mail this to his office with a note that says that his natural mother would like to see him."

Of course, Will had received the original message, which made him angry. Why in the world would someone claiming to be his real mother want to see him now? Did she need money? It set off a lot of confusion and angst that he thought he had put behind him as a teenager. After all, he was a successful attorney, why in the world would it matter to him? He had parents who loved him and supported him when he needed it. He didn't need her or her family.

When he received the crocheted square in the mail, his thoughts returned to his youth when he had wanted to know more about his biological parents. The yarn provided the evidence that this person was who she claimed to be. He justified his next action by being pragmatic. He would ask his adopted parents about the contact.

Perhaps, he should have information about his genetic makeup for health purposes.

Mary continued to telephone through the beginning of November. As a matter of fact, she became on first name basis with the gatekeeper secretary, Betty, who was an older woman.

One day, Betty said to Mary, "Boy you are a stubborn one. Maybe that runs in the family. I read that people get their intelligence from their mother that could apply to a stubborn streak too." Mary laughed. "Well, you know she did put me on this guilt trip."

They both chuckled. "I'll tell you what, if you stop calling, I promise I will talk to Will about it and get back to you." Betty said in a motherly tone.

"It's all I ask." Responded Mary.

After that telephone call, Mary reported the connection with Betty to Sophia, "But I would not be optimistic, Mama. He seems like he wants nothing to do with us. He will not even talk to me."

"I don't blame him," Sophia responded regretfully. "Promise me that you will continue to try after I am gone. Tell him about me, and his father." Each night Sophia told Mary a little more about her life growing up in the 1950s.

"Don't say that mama, we will get him to understand," Mary said with hope. She started to understand how very difficult life had been for her mother.

Betty eventually called Mary on the Tuesday before Thanksgiving. "He will consider the invitation. It's the best I can do," said Betty.

"I appreciate it, Happy Thanksgiving," responded Mary.

Sophia hid her disappointment when Mary told her, and continued to stare out the window at bare trees. Autumn was ending and winter beginning. Her health started to fail quickly.

Will did not come for Thanksgiving as invited. He did verify the facts with his adopted mother. He was angry that none of the information had ever been shared with him. Angry at his adopted parents, who he loved, angry at his natural mother, angry at the world. He hid it well and continued the routine of his single life. He had been an only child. His adopted parents could not afford to adopt any more children. They needed to keep the agreement with Sophia that they would send Bill to college.

Mary once left a message for Bill after Thanksgiving with Betty, his secretary. "Please tell him to call me." But he didn't return the call.

Around Christmas, Mary extended a party invitation to all family and friends. This time Will did come to Mary's house on Saturday before Christmas, which happened to be Christmas Eve.

He was hesitant as he approached the door of the middle class home but decided to push the doorbell anyway. He arrived a little before the official party time so as not to be awkward in front of other people. He could not understand why a private meeting had not been arranged, which made him a bit annoyed.

Mary's husband opened the door to see a well-dressed man in a cashmere coast with an expensive suit underneath and an ornate bottle of wine in his hand. "Well you must be Will. Mary said she invited you. Since you are the only person I don't recognize, it must be you" he said with a wide grin and an excitement that was almost contagious but made will feel uneasy. "Come in, come in", he repeated. "We are not quite ready, you are a little early but hey, is anyone ever ready for Christmas. So much to do. Everyone pitches in. Let me take your coat."

"No," Will strained his reply. "I'm not staying long." His eyes darted around as he saw children chasing through the house, shouting merrily. He had missed that in his own childhood. No one to run and play with at home. It was like a stab in the chest but he sat down anyway.

"Mary! Mary! Will's here," Mary's husband called, trying to avoid the terseness of the stranger. As Mary came in the room, Bill blurted "So let's get this over with, where is your mother?"

Mary sat quietly, opposite him as she said. "I am so sorry, Will. Mama died after Thanksgiving. I thought you knew." Mary's eyes reddened as she wringed her hands. "I thought I told Betty when I telephoned and left a message to call me. I am so sorry, so much was going on at the time. I forget exactly what I said."

Will's face lit up with anger as he rapidly rose. "Then why did you invite me here?"

"You are my brother, Will. Mama loved you in her own way. She wanted to explain. We know that it hard but hope that you can find it in your heart to understand her reason for the choice she made.

I promised Mama I would continue to be here for you and when you wanted, you would be part of our family. More than anything Mama wanted you to be part of our family for Christmas." Mary was not sure he had even heard her, as he flew out of the room, down the hall, and out the door in such a hurry.

His anger surged further. *How dare life hold out an offer and snatch it away.*

He had gone there to encounter his mother about his abandonment and she abandoned him once more.

Mary did not give up. She waited for a few months. Although Will did not take her calls, she persisted. She sent a formal invitation for him, and his adopted parents, to join her along with the entire extended family for an Easter luncheon at her home.

Again, Will showed up at the doorstep with an expensive bottle of wine, but dressed a little more casually. This time Mary made sure that she greeted him herself and hugged him when they greeted. He sat down at the table with 19 other people, feeling a bit uncomfortable. So much confusion as food passed from hand to hand around the table. His adopted parents had also accepted the invitation to support him. These people were his family. Mary's sisters and their husbands and partners, their children, all strangers who were related to him.

At the beginning, welcoming Will at dinner, and accepting him as member of the family, was something they did for their mother. At his first dinner, Will's nerves got the best of him and he almost dropped the gravy boat spilling dark brown liquid on the white table cloth. He tried hide his anxiety behind his napkin. The love he felt is what he had wanted all his life, a full family. Although the adults let Will express his emotion without comment, Mary's youngest son Tommy said "Don't be nervous, Uncle Will. You're a guest, mom will clean it up. It happens to everyone at least once. You don't have to eat asparagus. Here, have a piece of ham." Will smiled in spite of himself. His heart was home. He found the full family that he had missed as a child. They came to like, even love, Will.

God knows that he made up for all the lost time on every Christmas afterward. He became the favorite uncle of all time. Mary kept her promise to her mother, Sophia. Will had a family for that holiday, for Christmas, and every day for the rest of his life. And in turn, Will found what he missed.

In years to come, he grew the family with his own wife and children. As a full-fledged member of the family, he dutifully hosted the family Christmas party every 4th year. He never served asparagus.

Day 9:
Santa's Helpers

"My help is from the Lord."
- Psalm 121:2

God is so mean! Fighting to hold back the tears, Sally put on her brave face. She knew why her father had called a family meeting. A week had passed since Thanksgiving dinner and her mother was still in bed sick. God is so mean to make her mother suffer. God is so mean to break her father's heart. God is so mean to disrupt her entire family. Cancer is a terrible disease. Being nine years old proved to be way tougher than she thought it would be. Through her anger, she looked sideway at her father who also looked unhappy, with a deep frown across his face. She pushed back her long sandy brown hair away from her face. She ran her fingers through it nervously.

Her father called a family meeting without her mother present. Sally knew that the news was bad. Sally had a sinking feeling in the pit of her stomach when the three of them sat down to dinner. Her father turned off the television.

"Sally ...Tommy," she heard her father's voice in a distance through her thoughts. "This year, what we want most from Santa Claus is for Mommy to be well, right?" His eyes glistened and mouth trembled. Sally was a little afraid, she had never seen her father so upset. Maybe it was about the telephone call he had gotten from Mummie's doctor today. Sally watched Tommy's golden curls bobbed up and down on his four year old head as he nodded. He loved his Mommy "the most" he would say. He knew she had been sick, no one told him how to make her better, but if Daddy said Santa could do it, he believed him. Sally understood. She was not sure that Tommy would understand why Santa Claus could not visit their house this year. She would give anything if their mother would be better. Yet her thin old wool coat was small for her. A new one would be ever so helpful against the cold winter weather. She wistfully admired a beautiful jacket sitting in the store window.

As she walked home from school every day after she got off the bus. She would look so cool sporting the golden green jacket with a faux fur trimmed hood and matching gloves.

She felt horrible that she had feelings of selfishness. Yet, after all she had done this year to be helpful to her mother and father, she thought Santa Claus would have noticed. She held her brown eyes steady and face emotionless as her father spoke to them.

"Will Santa make Mommy better?" Tommy asked, wanting to make sure that Santa protected his mother. "We can't be sure, but we need to do everything we can so that Mommy is well." Her father tried again to explain to Tommy. "Santa Claus will not be visiting us this year, sweetie."

"Not even a stocking?" Tommy whined.

"Tommy, it's for Mummie!" Sally exclaimed. Then she felt sorry she was not more patient with her little brother as Tommy whimpered.

Their father gathered them into his arms for a group hug. "I am sure there might be a stocking or something, Santa would not forget you altogether." His mind raced as he wondered how he would manage to get away to even buy the smallest of items for Santa to give. Then there was the problem of the additional cost of gifts as a strain on their on their finances. He already walked a balance beam of work and meeting his wife's medical appointments and care. Poor man, his cheeks were sunken in from lack of sleep as huge dark rings surrounded his eyes. Yet, he counted his blessings. His occupation provided the technology to work remotely. His flexible schedule allowed him to attend each radiation treatment after the mastectomy. He wanted his wife to know he was in the battle with her against breast cancer.

He did hire support too. He had groceries delivered and people clean once a week. He also counted his blessing that his employer provided insurance. Medical and caregiving bills abounded. The payments and the paperwork kept him up some nights past midnight.

Thank goodness the children could go to school, be with friends, and get away a bit, he thought.

"If Mummie is not well enough to go to get a tree, perhaps Mrs. Price next door will visit with her for a while. We can go and surprise her. You know Mummie always liked to decorate the Christmas tree." Sally said hopefully. This gave Tommy a cause to smile. "Maybe", her father responded, "but I don't want to impose too much. Mrs. Price and the people from the church have already been very kind. They deliver meals during your mother's illness."

Then he pitched in "After all, Christmas is a time of love of the baby, Jesus, not only for presents and Santa Claus. I can look online to see if I can find a pageant or live nativity that we could see for free." It might help his wife to get out a bit too, even if she had to wear a bandana over her head. He watched Sally brightened up a bit.

"Sally, would you take this soup and toast to your mother?" Her father asked after Sally had finished eating. He had already started to clear the table and Tommy's job was to pick up his toys from the small living room floor.

For Thanksgiving, Mrs. Price delivered a turkey dinner with mashed potatoes and broccoli. Sally had attempted to make stuffing from a grocery store box. She always tried to add a little extra to make an event special. She had carefully cut some celery and onion to add to the mix. It had been very quiet event with the four family members circled around the humble wooden table. Her mother had only picked at the mashed potatoes, yet she vomited afterwards. She had been eating soup with soft vegetables every night for the last seven days. Sally didn't understand what radiation meant, but she knew it made her mother sick. Several months had passed since the first time she first overhead her parents. She did not understand what the diagnosis of breast cancer meant. She had gone to her room and looked at her own undeveloped chest wondering if she would get sick too someday.

She entered her parent's bedroom, "How are you feeling, Mummie?" Sally asked as she put the tray on the stand. Then she helped her mother sit up, fluffing her pillows.

"You are so sweet, Sally, I am not sure what I would do without you," her mother managed a weak smile. "I must have caught a bug the last time I went for treatment but I am feeling stronger."

"Mummie, daddy said he would look for a Christmas activity for us. Let him know when you might be able to go out a bit." Her mother chuckled "In my fashionable head bonnet?" Her mother raised her hand to the back of her head like a model would display a hat.

"Oh Mummie, no one cares about that anymore." Her mother reached out her arms and called Sally to her. "You are all the medicine I need, my sweet one." She hugged her. "Now Mummie, you need to eat to get your strength back." Sally noticed the blood had drained from her mother's face making her appear quite pale, like a ghost.

Her mother laid back against the pillow and smiled, then responded, "Yes, ma'am." Sally turned to get the food tray to put up on the bed.

She helped her mother hold the spoon and feed herself. "Silly me, I feel so weak".

"It will be okay, Mummie, you need more rest to recover from the treatments."

"Sally, I know that daddy was going to talk to you tonight about Santa Claus, and I am awfully sorry, honey." She managed to express while Sally continued to raise spoonful of food to her mouth.

"Mummie, I would like Tommy to have the waffle blocks that he wanted this year for Christmas. Daddy said Santa will not be able bring it for him, I would like to buy it. Do you think it would be alright to sell some of my things on eBay?"

"Sally that is a wonderful idea. But an entire waffle block set is awfully expensive. Maybe you and Tommy can clear out some of the toys for those less fortunate too." The idea seem to lift her mother's spirit in admiration for what a generous daughter she had raised. "Your father will not be able to help much." Her mother warned. "But I can manage to spare him to take you to the post office to ship items. Do you know how to sell items on EBay?"

"Sure, Mummie. I know I can find out." Sally felt pride in the conspiracy that she and her mother had created. They would bring Santa Claus even in the middle of the all the family problems. They huddled together and chatted about what Sally thought she might be able to let go. "May I sell the music box that Auntie gave me? Or the doll that Grandmother gave me when I was seven years old? I never played with it."

"Oh Sally, not that." Her mother said from time to time. Sally reassured her mother that she didn't want the items anymore and some other child might delight in it. Her mother finally gave in. They hugged each other tightly.

Her father came in the room. "What in the world are my girls up to?" Sally and her mother looked at each other and both said at the same time, "Nothing" with a slight snicker.

But after Sally had gone to bed, her mother and father spoke of the plan.

Her father doubted that Sally could make enough money. It was already so close to Christmas. But her mother convinced him that they should at least let her try. If it became too time consuming and her schoolwork fell behind, then they would let her know. He sincerely wanted to make his wife happy and he wanted to make Christmas a joy for their family. He felt that he was being pulled in too many directions. Everyone wanted a normal life. But nothing about fighting cancer is normal, for anyone, at any time of year.

When Friday night came and the weekend was full of promise, Sally took Tommy into the family room and sat him down on the chair. "Tommy, you want Santa to come to visit, right?"

Tommy brightened up. He wanted Santa to come more than anything.

"Well, this is what we need to do. We need to clean up the toys and give the best of what we have for other boys and girls to be able to play too." Tommy scratched his head. How did giving up his toys make Santa come to his house? "Well," Sally explained, "Santa might think that you have too much already so it is good to give to other children." Tommy finally agreed with the promise that Santa would do his best for a Christmas Eve visit to their house. Sally and Tommy went through all the toys that appeared to have promise to be able to sell.

The next Saturday, Mrs. Price visited with Sally's mother. Not only was she a neighbor, but they also were in the same prayer group. She had brought a casserole for the family. As she was leaving, she saw Sally staring diligently at her computer screen. On her way out, she addressed Sally who spewed out the whole story.

"Well, if the items do not sell on EBay, the church nursery would take them as a donation. You will not get money, but you never know, God sees everything" she said.

"Do you think so, about God seeing everything, I mean?" Sally asked.

Mrs. Price stopped in her tracks. After a pause she responded. "Yes," drew slowly from her lips. "Yes, Sally. In my mind, two things are true. God puts the right people in your life at the right time and God sees everything." She then turned and left the house.

Sally thought about it long and hard. Frustrated, she put everything away for the day, but the woman's words echoed in her mind, "God sees everything." Well, if God see everything then God knows I need help, Sally thought.

By the end of the week, she had only sold a couple of items for about $32.50. A far cry from the $60 she needed to buy Tommy the waffle block set that he wanted. Yes, being nine years old was proving to be hard. As a big sister, she could hardly bear the thought of the disappointment to her little brother. Santa Claus would not be coming after all to bring the toy he wanted. It was a week before Christmas and Sally related the news to her mother. "You tried very hard, sweetie. It would be very generous of you to donate the toys. You and Tommy agreed that you did not want them anyway. With the money you earned, your father can take you to the Dollar Store. Some decorations would be nice along with a few stocking stuffers for Tommy. At least it would be a Christmas surprise when he wakes up. Sally fell into her mother's arms, bemoaning in her mind of how she felt that the whole world was collapsing on her. She didn't say a word of it to her mother. The conspiracy failed. Would she lose her mother too? Her heart felt broken.

"Be brave, we should be hearing some good new soon." Her mother said to her.

Sally, Tommy, and her father gathered the unsold toys and took them to the church. In the lobby of the church was a giving tree. All the items on the tree were for children whose homes Santa would not be visiting. "Like us", said Sally.

"No." her father replied briskly, "We have each other and a little I put aside that I can spare. We are very blessed. We don't have everything that we want, but we have everything that we need."

"You're right, Daddy. We are a lucky family and if Mummie is well, we have everything we need." Responded Sally.

Sally did a small amount of decorating on her own around the house. She found artificial poinsettias from a couple years ago. The leaves were a bit faded so she colored them with red marker. Her father had managed to get a small artificial tree from Goodwill for $10. Christmas trees stringed with popcorn appeared in one of her music books. Well, if it was good enough then, it is good enough now. She strung the popcorn together and painted it gold. Sally scheduled a family tree decorating night. "What a clever idea", her mother commented upon seeing the popcorn garland. Her mother seemed to have a story about each old ornament they placed on the little tree. Between stories, they sang Christmas carols as they decorated.

Sally and her family attended services on Christmas Eve. Her mother saw almost everyone in her bible study class. They gathered around her to give their blessing and wish the family well.

Sally and Tommy still put out milk and cookies for Santa that evening, in case he could stop by. Their father put on his computer. For fun, NORAD tracked Santa. Sally and Tommy could see where Santa was stopping everywhere in the world. Sally moped, everywhere but her house.

Her mother seemed to have a bit more energy this evening. They gathered to listen while her father read aloud the poem, 'Twas the Night before Christmas.

"You know," her father said. "Saint Nicholas was a real person. He was a holy man called a Bishop, who lived a long, long, long time ago, a little over three hundred years after Jesus died. He loved doing good for other people and had a reputation for secret gift giving. You see, most of the time, we are the hands and feet of God. We are the people who give here on earth. We are the secret Santas." Her father gave Sally a wink.

Tucked in her bed that evening, Sally waited for her father. Tommy had fallen asleep while he was reading and he carried Tommy to his bed.

Sally felt lucky that she could do a little to make Tommy's Christmas happy. Her father acknowledged her efforts to make the holiday merry for the family. He entered her room. "Sweet Dreams and Merry Christmas." He said and kissed her on the forehead. Her heart swelled with love for him. She wanted her mother to be well more than anything in the world, so she fell asleep with a prayer on her lips. "Dear Lord. Make my mother well so we can be together, as a family for a long time."

Imagine her surprise on Christmas morning as she awoke to Tommy's shouts of excitement. She threw on her robe and ran downstairs. To her amazement there was a full live Christmas tree decorated with their ornaments! Under the tree were two big boxes, one for her and one for Tommy. "Mummie, daddy, come see", cried out Sally. But they were already standing in the hallway smiling.

Sally ripped open the package, there was the golden green jacket that she had longed for. Tommy sat admiring his new waffle block set. Sally ran to hug her mother and father.

But you didn't get anything," Sally said to her mother and father "It's okay, honey. We have each other and many more years together. Your mother got her report from the doctor yesterday. We wanted to wait until Christmas morning to tell you that your mother has overcome the cancer. She is on the way to recovery." Tommy was busy playing waffle blocks. He was building a road for the matchbox cars to travel on across the living room. He let out a whoop, "Hurray for Mommy!"

Sally put on her jacket, admiring it. She ran back to her mother and father and hugged them again, "This is the best Christmas ever." Sally exclaimed.

"But how did Santa's helpers know what I wanted? How did Santa stop at our house after all? How, how?" Sally kept asking. Her mother grinned, "The hand of God is so powerful that angels appear. God sees everything."

Day 10:
A Christmas Miracle

*"He who believes in me will live, even though
he dies, and whoever lives and believes
in me will never die."*

- John 11:21-24

Timothy *looks so peaceful, like he is asleep instead of in a medically induced coma,* Diana thought. She looked upon her college age son in the hospital bed surrounded by an assorted variety electronic machines providing life support. A head wrap protected the 26 wires of the EEG electrodes that sprouted from his head and detected electrical activity in his brain. She studied the wiggly electric black lines of the five frequency bands on the monitor with the hope that they would reveal the way for treatment.

Just last week she watched him playing on the

beach, throwing a football with a friend. His blonde hair and piercing blue eyes accented his healthy, strong, athletic appearance. This week, he was in a medical coma to keep him from seizing endlessly in a state called status epileptus. An unknown virus had attacked his nervous system. If the medical team could not break the action of the neurons that fired in one direction, rather than randomly as normal brains, he would surely die.

His condition confounded the neurologists as he was transferred from one hospital to another and to another.

He had his own nurse in the neuro intensive care unit but Diana felt that a mother's loving care would help reach him. First, the doctors had tried to identify the virus, but as days turned into weeks and weeks turned into months, it became less important of what caused the illness then trying to diagnose and treat it.

Finally he was transferred to a research hospital where Diana signed waivers almost daily for untested treatments. This medicine might make him go blind. *Ok, I might as well agree because what good was sight if he is dead,* so she signed it.

Another procedure needed her consent to allow

multiple IVs to be inserted. She signed it. No one knew what would save him. They kept trying and she continued to sign each and every consent put before her.

Diana prayed for her son's life each day with a rosary. Not only did she pray for her son's life, she created a time to have a full community prayer for him. At 12:15 PM each Friday, she called all her on her church, friends, her sons' friends, and her Facebook Community to pray for Timothy to live. She received prayers and well wishes from even people who claimed to be atheist. The heavens were flooded with the desire to return Timothy to life.

Not only the heavens, also cards and pictures of friends brought a comfort to the hospital room as Diana made an arch on the wall in front of his bed. She wanted love to surround him in the hope that some way, somehow, in his deep state of being, it would be able to reach him. He would know he was loved.

While she was not allowed to touch Timothy in his coma in the Neuro Intensive Care Unit of a traditional hospital, in the research facility a new doctor had given her permission to try alternative therapies. "We are way beyond the normal standard of care." One doctor told her, "Try anything, just let us know first."

Each Monday evening when she arrived, she would talk to Timothy as if he could hear her. After resting, she started reflexology of his feet and applied the essential oil, frankincense. She would start at the heel and move her fingers to the base of the big toe, which is supposed to be connected to the head. Then she applied an anti-toxin pad that was supposed to absorb the toxins in his body. She knew how crazy it sounded, but she was desperate to try anything. All the while, she sang and prayed for his recovery.

Nights in the neuro intensive care unit brought incidents of pain, people crying for help.

Since she slept in the hospital, by the window in Timothy's room, she saw and overheard a lot of pain of desperate people. Family members suffered the pain of loss. *If people could only see the pain their families suffered, they would show more love on a daily basis.* She often thought.

One night, around 2 AM, Diana awoke due to a loud commotion. She rose and went to the hallway. At the other end of the hallway, a medical team surrounded a gurney as it moved away from her toward a room. She yawned and stretched, then decided to go the restroom next to the lobby. Diana could not use the bathroom attached to where she slept due to potential infection.

On her way back, she saw a teenage girl with long dark brown hair that fell like a veil over herself. The girl curled up in a corner, shaking from head to foot. Diana could not help but stop and comfort her. "My brother is dying." She wept putting her head in Diana's shoulder. "I am so sorry", mumbled Diana. "What happened?" Between hard sobs the girl related the story of a car accident. "Where is your family?" Diana asked.

The young girl explained that they were all in the room with her brother. "That is really where you should be too," Diane said tenderly.

"I can't take it, I just can't take it!" the girl emphasized.

"But they will worry about you," Diana explained. "I am sure they want you with them to help them through this loss, to know their daughter is safe with them. It will comfort them."

Diana helped her find the room again. In fact, the relief on her parent's face showed as they hugged their daughter and kept their eyes on their dying son. Such a sad sight, Diana knew it was hard to watch such a young person die.

The pain in her own heart magnified.

Yet, to the outside world she continued her daily routine with hope. She never let anyone know the pain she carried. She felt that she did not have the right to give into despair. Her reasoning centered on the tragedy that surrounded her.

Once she had once walked into the hospital lobby and looked up to a mounted television. A news report stated that a young high school student had died practicing football that day. His parents did not have the opportunity to fight for him. They never knew that they would never be able to tell him how much they loved him. God gave her the opportunity to fight for her son. An opportunity that some parents, like the young man in the car accident, did not have. An opportunity like the young man playing football that day did not have. So she did not have the right to show the same pain, she thought.

On Timothy's 22nd birthday, about two months into the medical coma, the entire family gathered at the hospital to say goodbye to him and celebrate his life. Diana bought him miniature hot wheels car that looked like the Mustang he used to drive. John, his oldest brother, brought him a Lighten McQueen helium balloon that floated over his bed stating, "Happy Birthday." Guy, Diana's middle son, gifted him a book by comedian Jim Belushi. Guy would read out loud to Timothy resulting in entertainment for the nursing staff, too.

However, one particular neurologist warned her. If he survived, he might not be able to move. They didn't know what type of neurological damage had been done. He might only be able to blink.

"Mum, would Tim really want to live that way?" John asked.

"I'm not sure, but do I have the right to cut off his life because he might not be able to move? Look at Stephen Hawkins, he has lived a productive life," she said through her tears.

"You know we will continue to support you as long as you want to fight but don't think of it as a failure if he does not live," said Guy. "It's something we have to face."

Timothy's father had nothing to add. Emotional suffering distorted the expression on his face. He had avoided coming to the hospital to face this moment but could avoid it no longer. He had to take the chance to say goodbye to his son while Timothy was still alive.

She decided to continue to fight. Since she had been told from a nurse that, anecdotally, patients who had someone visiting or attending them while in a coma had a higher chance of recovery, Diana continued to stay in the hospital with her son during the week. After work on Monday, she traveled 150 miles to the hospital and slept there, on a cold plastic mattress until she left on Thursday. She would travel the 2.5 hours to her home to work on Friday and rest on the weekend only to start the next week in the same manner. The routine was wearing but she continued day after day. When she was not in the hospital room with him, she would take a break to the lounge to catch up on some work, visit the cafeteria, or pray in the chapel.

On Friday, Saturday, and Sunday, Timothy's brothers John and Guy, performed the vigil so that Diana could rest. Timothy had someone from his family with him every day, talking to him, reading to him, or just being with him.

By the end of Thanksgiving holiday the decision of whether he lived or died appeared out of her control. Over Thanksgiving dinner, they started to talk about potential burial plans for Timothy.

"Do you know if Tim wanted to be buried or cremated?" John asked.

"Once when we were watching a horror movie, the plot required a body to be exhumed. He had stated that he did not want to turn into a lump of glob similar to buried bodies that had been filled with embalming fluids. I would say that indicated that he would want to be cremated," Diana replied.

"Where do you plan to bury him?" Guy piped in.

"I've given it a bit of thought and I want to ask if he could be included in the burial plot with his grandparents. If he is cremated the urn would not take up much room," Diana responded.

"I will look into it," said John.

November turned into December.

One Sunday, Diana got a strange feeling. She called to see if her son had visited Timothy that day. She found out that he had but he had left early. She called the nurse's desk to see what was going on. The doctor had ordered an MRI.

"But he cannot have an MRI if he has the EEG leads on, right?" Diana asked.

"The EEG was taken off his head before they took him down," The nurse responded.

Now Diana was sure something was going on, she jumped in her car and drove the 2-1/2 hours to her son's bedside only to see the lights blazing in his shut eyes. She turned off the lights and put up a sign saying:

"Seizure patient, keep lights off. If lights required, cover his eyes."

She laid down on the plastic mattress, fully dressed, and went to sleep.

At 5 AM the next morning, she caught the head epileptologist, for the first and only time in the entire time Timothy had been in the Neuro ICU.

He, along with an entourage of medical students, was heading out the door as she awoke. She ran after him. "Doctor, doctor, why was the EEG taken from Timothy's head?" she asked as she made her way through the students that followed him down the hall.

"We think we know enough about his condition at this point," The doctor replied.

"So what is the next step?" She persisted.

"If the hospital diseases haven't killed him yet, we will give it a little more time." The doctor, with his entourage, disappeared into the next patient's room. Diana dared not to follow, she stood motionless and speechless.

True. He suffered from hospital pneumonia at the end of November. Diana had stayed by his bedside cleaning his trachea tube so he could breathe. She would take the congested slime out of the tube as fast as she could and reinsert it like the nurses taught her.

Every ten minutes, or so, she removed the tube to clean it. The congested green material would shoot out the hole in his throat across the room as he coughed. It reminded her of the scene from The Exorcist. She felt that she was fighting the devil himself. Her grandfather had died of hospital pneumonia. She knew how dangerous the infection could be.

Her encounter with the epileptologist was on the 17th of December. She stayed with Timothy for several days afterward and left when John arrived to relieve her of hospital duty.

As he hugged her, John insisted she get some rest, "You look tired, Mum. Get a good meal, I know you don't get to eat well at the hospital."

By the 23rd, Diana receive a telephone call from him while she was at work.

"Mum, are you ready for this?" her son asked cautiously

Diana braced herself, "Go on."

"Timothy is awake and wants to see you." He said hesitantly. "But he can't move his body whatsoever, he can only blink yes or no."

She only heard, he is awake. "He is awake." She shouted.

"It's a miracle, a Christmas miracle." She fell backward in her chair, then raised again in a dance for joy.

"Is it?" John insisted. "I told you, he can only open his eyes."

"Let's accept the miracle that is granted today. To me, it's a miracle. God will reveal the full miracle in time. After months of prayer, Timothy is awake. For that, I am thankful for the opportunity to continue the struggle," she replied. "I'm on my way to the hospital."

She drove home and grabbed her packed bag. Before the long drive she signed onto her internet account and reported the miracle online for all to see. Timothy was awake for Christmas.

He had opened his eyes, he was out of the

medical coma. She spread the word of the Christmas miracle far and wide.

John was right. Timothy's struggle had only began as he fought to resurrect himself from a deathlike state of being. He weighed under 80 pounds, half the weight of when he was stricken. He appeared like a skeleton, his bones showing through his flesh.

He was alive but he couldn't move. His muscles had atrophied over the four months that he had been in a coma.

With only three more days until Christmas, Diana reached out to all for the prayer warriors. She asked their prayers that her son would continue to improve for the recovery miracle she sought.

Until she arrived at the hospital, John continued to ask Timothy questions with a blink once for "yes" and blink two for "no." He seemed to be responding to the point that he was aware of what was happening around him.

Upon the arrival at the hospital, she started the trek to the Neuro ICU. It always seemed like a quest for her to conquer. Turn left at the golden leaves, go up the elevator, proceed down the hall and turn right at the silver globe. Go over the bridge and up another elevator, then arrive.

Upon entering the room, she hugged John tightly and kissed his cheek to thank him for taking care of his brother. Then she went over to Timothy to hold his hand while he slept.

On Christmas day, the two brother and mother surrounded Timothy with enthusiasm for a new life. It was the happiest Christmas that Diana ever had, even if it was in a hospital room eating an overcooked turkey dinner with salty stuffing. Her joy of being with her sons outshone all other joys, no matter the quality of food. They rejoiced in their perseverance that reached the young man in a coma, thought to be dead, rendered back to life.

That evening, she could hear Timothy trying to move as she slept in the cold window seat area of his room. She woke with a fright that he was having a seizure. Every time she would go to his bed, she would ask him, did you do that on purpose. He blinked once for yes. "Please let's get some sleep." She responded. But he would do it again, and again. He was anxious to get back to life.

Their family received a miracle for Christmas.

She didn't know why, but she would accept God's grace as it was bestowed.

She would keep fighting for what she could control and leave the rest to God.

The doctors continued to warn her, "His organs may fail or malfunction due to the prolonged period of coma." But Timothy continued to improve.

The hospital counselor presented her with an hour long session of the psychological effects of brain trauma. She asked, "Is this what I should expect for his future behavior?"

The counselor responded, "We don't know. We have never had anyone wake up from this type of situation before."

During his recovery in the hospital, Timothy maintained his sense of humor. He begged passersby to come into his room and visit. He would call out to the nurses in the hall or anyone who he happened to see to come to give him a hug.

In years to come, the nurses of the neuro ICU encouraged other families with Timothy's story. "Once we had a patient who woke up after four months of a medically induced coma, don't give up hope. Miracles happen, especially at Christmas."

Day 11:
A Pandemic Christmas

"You shall love your neighbor as yourself."
– Mark 12:31

Month after month dragged on and on. Every day like the day before. It seemed like forever that Don had not had real human contact. The COVID-19 virus had struck at the hearts and drove fear into many people, including him. He wasn't as much in fear of getting sick himself, he was only 34 years old. He was afraid of giving it to his family, especially his grandparents. He didn't want to be the person to transmit a virus that could kill them. His family would excommunicate him. He could hear it all now, they lived through World War II but could not survive their grandson's loneliness. He knew if he stayed quarantined that it was unlikely they he would contract the virus or give it to anyone else.

So he stayed inside, most of the time, away from others. Almost nine months had past. He quarantined himself in his 960 square foot apartment that grew to feel like a prison. He hated to watch the news, but he found he needed to know how bad it the situation effected everyone.

The streets were empty with a bizarre feel that humankind had abandoned the world. If he didn't know better, he would have thought he was in one of the odd episodes of the old black and white film series, The *Twilight Zone*. He thought of the episode where a bomb had killed most the people but left the buildings intact. His fascination with these old reruns was like his addiction to watching the news. Binge watching it for several hours was part of his day.

Maybe he wouldn't be so lonely if he had been able to make his relationship work. He and his girlfriend had come to an understanding. After a little over 30 days quarantined together in his cramped space, they agreed that they were not a match. She left, and it crushed his soul. He believed that everything happened for the best. At least he found out early in the relationship that they were not right for each other.

Weeks before Christmas, Don put up an artificial Christmas tree that he kept in the storage unit. He laughed when his mother gave it to him several years ago. "You never know when you might need an extra Christmas tree."

He managed to salvage some decorations and made ornaments from old pictures to hang on the tree. He figured if he couldn't physically be with his family, at least they could be with him symbolically. Stores were open and he had picked up some ribbon and glued the loop to the object to hang it. He could do that because he had little else to do during the day.

For the first several months, he tried going to the restaurant that he managed at least two times a week to see if he could stir up some business. The restaurant was family owned, the owner was his boss. He liked to mingle with guests, not work, so he had made Don the manager. It was almost like family. He missed it.

The state government officials had closed all restaurants to indoor and outdoor dining. His boss, and the head cook handled the little bit of takeout business. His visit grew less often as the quarantine lingered. Still, at least once a month he would make a trip through the city to the restaurant. His boss would give him a free meal, sealed, and sanitized.

Everyone quarantined. He thought by putting up a Christmas tree it would lift his spirits, give him hope. After all, rumors of a vaccine were in the horizon.

His mother generally woke him up with a telephone call to say good morning. He and his friends would have cocktails together via Zoom at 6 on a regular basis. The personal contact was sorely lacking but at least he could communicate with someone once a day if he planned it out right.

After TV time in the morning, he would go out for a walk to stretch his long lanky legs. Almost no one else out participated. Sometimes he would see someone walking their dogs. They always stayed six feet away and it was hard to talk or engage with someone with a mask on. He counted himself lucky if he got a brief wave.

Christmas lost a lot of the magic that radiates with the season of love. No celebrations, no church, no family would fill his heart with joy. The Grinch had somehow stolen Christmas and little Cindy-Sue was nowhere in sight to save it. He was truly depressed but resisted taking the medication that his doctor had prescribed.

He somewhat envied his brother and sister in law. At the beginning of the pandemic, they moved themselves, and their two children, out of the city into their parent's home in suburbs. He wished he could do it too but he knew the strain would be too much for his folks.

At his parent's house, they would open gifts on Christmas Eve. Each year Santa would make an appearance as his father disappeared from sight. He was pretty sure his niece and nephew knew that it was their grandfather, but they enjoyed the fun anyway.

That suit must be over 40 years old by now, he smiled to himself. He remembered his dad doing the same thing when he was a child. He would miss it, the pain of exclusion tore at his heart. Sure, they would meet via Zoom, but it wouldn't be the same.

Don's mother called Christmas Eve morning, "Hello darling, what do you have planned for yourself today?"

Don replied, "Same old, same old. I thought we could Zoom when we opened gifts tonight. Did you receive everything I ordered for the family off of Amazon?" He asked.

One blessing that Don felt was that he received unemployment compensation. He could afford his rent and Christmas presents. He considered himself lucky because he had some friends that were financially struggling.

"That was so sweet of you. Yes, we received something for everyone. Thank you so much. The kids are driving your father crazy. He is building something in the backyard so they can go out and play a bit more. I wish you could be with us tonight Don, but we are almost at the end of the quarantine, I would hate for anything to happen now," his mother said weakly.

"I understand Mum, I truly do." He lifted his voice to try to sound cheerful, but his voice cracked with emotion.

"I love you," she added.

"Love you too. Mum, talk to you tonight," he replied.

Don turned on the TV as usual, another rerun of the *Twilight Zone* started. He played around about an hour making another ornament for the Christmas tree then an unexpected ring of the telephone took him off guard.

"Don, Don, are you there?" He recognized the voice and his heart skipped a beat.

"Yeah, boss, I'm here. Glad to hear your voice, what's up?"

"Don, we have more takeout orders than I can handle. I think that business is picking up. I hate to put you in this position, but would you possibly consider coming back to work? We have instituted all the CDC guidelines. I need you, but if you don't feel comfortable with working at this point, I can call one of the other crew members. "

"Are you kidding? I can be there in an hour," replied Don but before he could say good bye, his boss interrupted.

"One more thing Don, I can't pay you your regular salary until indoor dining returns."

Ouch, that hurt. Don's unemployment check was almost as much as his pay with the extra federal funding provided. Still he responded, "Um, ok, we can work out something. I would like to get back to work." He felt if he didn't get some personal contact again he would lose his mind.

Back to work, on Christmas Eve, it felt like a miracle. Don mouthed the words, *Thank you, God, Thank you, God* as he quickly looked up to heaven and folded his hands in prayer. People going out, people overcoming fear to be together in some way. He was elated.

He threw his clothes on and ran to catch a bus to the restaurant. Masks, yes, take several so he could sanitize and change them. Take some plastic zip lock bags to put the masks into so he could wash him. If his luck held out, maybe the shutdown would soon be over.

As he arrived at the restaurant, the owner waved him back as Don moved forward to give him a welcoming embrace. He chuckled to himself, "Wow, yeah, even the most innocent movements have to be muted to conform."

"You got that right, we can't afford for anyone to get sick, they will shut us down for sure," said his boss who then elbow bumped him in a playful way. "It's a little awkward. We have to take several more steps than you remember to make sure everything stays sanitized, but hey, we are here, right?" His boss gave him a wink.

They worked all day, making sure that all

members were six feet apart. No one took breaks with each other, everyone needed to stay separate but coordinate together.

The takeout meal was sealed after cooked so the food was never touched after it left the stove.

Yet, Don enjoyed each and every telephone call. He used a UV light to sanitize the phone after each call ended and various surfaces he touched.

By 6 PM that evening, the meals had been distributed and his boss gave Don a meal to go for himself. "Available tomorrow?" asked his boss.

"Working on Christmas day this year boss?" Don asked puzzled.

"Well, you know we haven't in the past, but this year was so tough, Don, If there are orders coming in, I will need you," his boss replied

"I have no important plans anyway. I will be here," answered Don.

Don looked at the owner, who appeared to have shrunk from stress. His shoulders stooped His head bent over. Even the loans the federal government made were not enough to keep the restaurant alive. He knew the man dug deep into his own savings. The two men looked into each other's eyes and saw the toll this virus and shutdown had taken.

Don picked up his meal and decided that he would walk home through the brisk air. It felt good. As he approached his building, he saw one string of lights on the balcony beside his window. He decided to knock on his neighbor's door.

"Mrs. Wilson, are you home?" Don shouted.

A faint grandmother voice responded through the door. "I am, but I am not taking any visitors because of the Covid 19 virus."

Don lit up with an idea, "Mrs. Wilson, It's Don, your next door neighbor. I have a Christmas Eve meal that I brought from the restaurant where I work. I'll leave it outside your door so you can enjoy it."

"How sweet of you, you don't have to do that, dear," said the old lady.

"Mrs. Wilson, get the food and let's sit out on our balconies together to enjoy Christmas Eve."

Don scrambled inside and took out the meal that he had previously prepared for the evening. He heated it up quickly. When he went outside, he could see that Mrs. Wilson had retrieved the meal from outside her door and had it on a little table facing his balcony ready to eat.

"Mmm, this is delicious, you didn't have to do

this." Mrs. Wilson muttered again through the next bite.

"Mrs. Wilson, it's Christmas Eve, how long has it been since you have seen friends or family. Not a caregiver, but someone to enjoy conversation with? Mrs. Wilson, I am delighted that you can join me." Don never thought those words would ever come out of his mouth. He and Mrs. Wilson didn't exactly get along. She reported him often to building management for playing music too loud. Here he was, starved for direct human contact. He opened Christmas Eve to spend with her.

"My daughter worries about me you know. She lives so far away. I wish it were different. She wanted me to go stay in a nursing home so I would be with other people to care for me. Can you imagine that? Well, I don't trust those places. I like my own home better. She checks on me daily by telephone. I miss her." Her lips pursed as the words became barely audible. "Enough of that," she quickly recovered from her depression and continued to eat.

The two chatted as they ate. Mrs. Wilson told stories to Don of Christmas' past with her husband and family. He shared equally amusing tales of toys that were popular when he was growing up, especially the Rock'em Sock'en robots. Don poured himself more wine not wanting the time to end.

As she spoke, he saw the release of Mrs. Wilson's tense facial expressions which mirrored all the worries, anxieties, and fears of his own family members. He felt he could understand a bit better that, although he had been lonely, it was tougher on the older generation who did not feel as comfortable with electronic communications.

Around 8 PM, he heard his telephone ring. "Mrs. Wilson, I am opening presents with my family via Zoom."

"Oh my Lord, what will they think of next?" she almost squealed

"Do you have any presents to open? Would you like to join us?" Don asked.

"My gracious. yes. I did save a couple things under the tree that my daughter and grandchildren sent. I will speak to them tomorrow but we didn't plan to share the gift opening. I would love to join you."

She went inside her apartment to get a bit warmer. She replaced her ugly Christmas sweater she had worn with a dark red wool jacket, then came back out with a couple small gifts.

Don introduced her to his family, and although the balcony space made the computer screen small, she could hear their laughter and joy as they experienced Christmas remotely together.

The Christmas magic returned to Don's heart. Don now felt the true purpose of Christmas was love. The Christmas spirit was a special sharing time; sharing with family, sharing with friends, and sharing with neighbors. It is never too late to open your heart to let the magic pour in.

Don drank another glass of wine after he ended the Zoom call with his family and said his final "Merry Christmas" to Mrs. Wilson. He didn't fall asleep until about 1 AM. It was no longer Christmas Eve, but Christmas Day.

He thought he heard jingle bells at midnight and spent a long time looking out the window at the world outside. Perhaps the jingle bells told him that Saint Nicholas had visited. Maybe Santa had hit that mean old Grinch with a huge present to get him to open up his heart too, he chuckled to himself. All it took for Don was human contact.

He looked forward to going to work, like he had never before.

Above all, he looked forward to the New Year.

The world would recover from the deadly threat of the virus that knocked us all down, but could not steal the love of the Christmas season away. Thank you God, praised his soul as he fell into a deep sleep to awaken to a new day.

Day 12:
La Befana - The Old Woman of Christmas

"No longer a servant. I call you friend."
- John 15:15

BEFANA AWOKE BEFORE THE rooster crow to another ordinary day in the Roman province of Judea. Weariness seized her from her late work the night before. She forced her old bones to move out of the bed. She was annoyed with life, the lost dreams of a young girl hidden in the furthermost corners of her mind. She wore rags, no one minded because no one cared about her. She was only another household asset that did her job and kept to herself. The other slaves were much younger. They avoided the old hag as privileged to do much lighter work. She didn't mind. She went to the well, as usual, and drew the water she needed and started her daily routine, cleaning. She was one of the few servants that cleaned the ground by wiping the stone with the wet rags after she thoroughly swept with her broom. She let out a groan as she knelt on the cold stone. Sometimes she would slump to the ground, crawling, inadvertently cleaning it with her skirt.

Her one release of the dreariness of her day in Bethlehem was to go to the marketplace for fresh vegetables for the household. Her master allowed her do this because she had a sharp nose and a keen sense of smell to determine ripeness. Besides, he figured the old slave had nowhere to run, so his asset was safe. It was a privilege granted because of the remote location. She never would have been able to do so in Rome. And when they returned to Rome after her master's time in Bethlehem attending to the census was over, she would miss it tremendously.

When she went to the market on this particular day, the crowd of people circled like ants on an ant hill, busy going about their work. So many strangers flocked into Bethlehem due to the census. She was shoulder to shoulder with them, barely budging through the crowd. She stopped at the first vendor for figs. She heard a buzz of gossip from one stand to another. The vendor said to her, "What does your master make of the bright light in the evening. Is it favorable to Rome? You must over hear something in the household." But Befana turned away without a word. Everyone was talking about the evening sky and the bright light that had started to appear, growing stronger each evening. Speculations flew about the meaning. Good for Rome? Good for Judea? What sign did the star bring? Befana dismissed it as unimportant. It was an ordinary day for Befana, which would transform into an extraordinary night.

That evening, as the cool wind blew and the stars shone, three men of various ages wandered through the narrow roads of the small town of Bethlehem. Royal garb of purple, gold, and blue, peeked out from under their dark cloaks. They looked up, up, up at the patterns of stars that illuminated in the night sky.

Despite their age difference, they had been friends for years. Their friendships extended back many years to the time that they met studying astronomy at the Library in Alexandria. Caspar's white beard betrayed him as the eldest in age. He was well known for his wisdom in his home country, Persia. Melchior, whose hailed from Arabia, was twenty years his junior. His complexion was a little darker. His face sported a dark beard that had a streak of gray hair. Both of them were like fathers to the youngest member of their troop. Balthasar carried very dark skin from Ethiopia. Although the color of their skins greatly varied, they could not have closer than if they had been born into the same family. They bonded to each other through the love of the stars and the Spirit that guided the universe from which the stars shone.

For months, they, and several other companions who accompanied them to be of service, had followed a bright light illuminating the night sky.

As astronomers they studied the night sky and believed it to be a foretelling of a great event, the coming of a king. They knew not the cause of the light, the travelers followed in faith.

The men carried the dirt of the days and the miles they traveled. Even their beasts of burden, a camel and two horses seemed to resist traveling any further.

Caspar murmured to Balthasar that he felt they were close. Melchior agreed as they proceeded through the star lit street.

Melchior pointed to an estate at end of the street that still shone a light. By the size of the estate, this was a prominent Roman household. Someone might have more information of the events in the area. They passed through the gate to a tiny hovel serving as a gatehouse that blocked strangers from entering without notice.

There, sweeping this late hours was a bent over form, a woman beaten down by life. Her shoulders slumped, a scar across her face. Befana stood before them, cleaning as usual, taking pride in being the best house keeper her master kept in service. She had been a slave since she was sold at five years old to pay her family's debt. She knew nothing but work before her. When she was young, she served as a concubine, but that stopped years ago. She had been promised that she could buy her freedom after 50 years of service.

Although she had earned enough money to do so, she failed to take the opportunity. Being a slave was all she knew. She was then sold again to the appointed official that was to help take the census in this remote Roman province. That is how she ended up in this god's forsaken place, she thought. She spit on the gods of her youth. Zeus showed no pity for her, Hera never provided a home. She was disgusted from abuse and her heart was hard.

She saw the three royals approaching from the corner of her eye but paid little mind to them. She did not consider that they would stop to speak to a lowly servant. They were not her masters. She worked hard enough and she turned her back.

Caspar approached the doorway and called out to the woman, "We have journeyed far and almost at the end. A miracle event is happening. Look at the sky this evening and see the brightness that makes it look like day. The bright light has lead us this far but local guidance would be appreciated. Surely you might have heard of a remarkable event." They repeated the question asked many times before, "Where is he who has been born King of the Jews? "

She had learned the hard way to keep her nose out of the household business. She had been whipped and beaten for speaking improperly to members of the Roman family. Across her face she carried the scar of a blow delivered by her master for perceived insolence.

She acted as if she did not hear them. They should not be speaking to her anyway.

But Caspar persisted. "Old lady, get your master. We would like information. We need to know about an event of the coming of a king."

She remembered the marketplace gossip from that day but nothing about a King. The people had wondered. Was that why the vendor asked about what her master thought of the sign? She dared not say what the people might speculate.

Impatient at their insistence, she screeched, "I don't know, let me alone. This is a Roman household. I have no king but Caesar."

Melchior continued, "But you must have heard or seen something, anything that might indicate where he is."

"If I did it would be treasonous to do so. I have

no king but Caesar and you would disgrace our household if I let you past to see my master."

Melchior changed the tone of his voice and pursued gently. We look for the coming of the King who would bring freedom to his people, open a new period of hope, peace, joy, and love. It will set people free, no longer slaves, a new age. You may have heard rumors.

The old woman seldom thought about her oppression, her tolerance for it had grown over time. But this talk of freedom sparked in her the ideas from youth of leaving this life of a slave. She looked around her hovel. Nothing held her there but her fear.

Caspar persisted, "Perhaps if you know something you might join us. Come with us. We do not know the way. If you guide us, we will return to pay your master for your freedom in the morning. Come take your freedom."

Freedom, the word seemed to make her head swarm. The woman dared not to take that step. She had been a slave too long and knew no other life. If they had only come 10 years ago she would have been strong enough.

Curiosity struck Befana. Her voice crackled, "I

cannot go with you but I can offer a place for you to rest for a while and water for your animals. Tell me more about the king you seek."

Caspar sat down slowly, feeling his age down to his very bones. "I suffer the pain of old age, perhaps you do also. But the hope of aiding the dawn of a new age that will break this age of barbarism, to help humanity to recognize love for one another drives me on to my task. We have gathered three royal gifts in accordance with the proper gifts for a king, for we know not what we will find."

Balthasar, being young and energetic, had brought the gifts in to where they rested and, when asked, displayed them for Befana. "Behold, gifts for a king; Gold, myrrh, and frankincense." Melchior explained further, "Gold for the recognition of a king. Myrrh for the mortality of the divine made human. Frankincense that serves to heal and raise when burnt to praise God."

Their talk of one God, a loving God, who wanted salvation for humankind mesmerized Befana. What a different thought this was from the worship of gods that never seemed satisfied with the sacrifices she presented and rendered to her this dreadful life. Her gods fought with each other. Their stories told of conflict between divine beings that interacted with humans, bringing pain. No peace seemed to reign under them. A child had been born to change all that, a child anointed by the one God, a Christ child.

After several hours, the men rose to leave. She could see the toil of travel having taken its toll on all of them but also saw the determination, inspired by faith, in their faces.

Melchior looked upon the dirty, old woman, missing several teeth, trapped in the life she had always known. "Will you come with us to freedom?" Melchior extended his hand.

The question startled Befana because the thought had been sitting in the back of her mind from the very first moment they had asked her to be their guide. She hesitated, she could not leave everything she knew all her life. It meant that she would have to trust these strangers who spoke words of hope but may cut her throat as soon as she left safety. She grieved that her fear immobilized her and let the terror in her heart keep her bound as her head flopped in a motion that moved from left to right and back again. "No, I will remain with the familiar." The old woman picked up her broom and started to clean again.

Disappointed, they retreated from the small house and left her to finish her task.

Pulling the door behind him as they departed, Balthasar looked at the old woman mournfully. Later, each man discussed the Befana's sad situation. They felt, in a way, that they had failed to convince her of her value. From what she had told them of her master, Melchior stated that Befana was most probably correct, a Roman official would not help them to find a new king.

But as she swept she began to sob, a little at first and then harder. Her mind filled of thoughts that Caspar spoke, an age when people were free, no longer slaves. An age when compassion for another human would prevail and love find a way. The images of the men pressed in her brain in a way she could not shake. Their words repeating again and again, no longer a slave, free and equal in the eyes of the one God.

After several hours of allowing their talk of freedom to fill her heart with desire for the life that she always wanted, but was afraid to pursue, she ran out to the middle of the street to call after the

Hoping that they had stopped again not far away to ask another she cried out, "Come back! Come back! I have changed my mind. I will go with you to find the child that you seek, the king that will bring joy to the world. Please come back!"

A scream that turned into plead. "Please, come back." She repeated it again and again, each time her voice fading a bit more, finally to a quiet whisper. She covered her face with her calloused hands and fell to her knees.

The three wise men, and their companions, had gone on their way. They were no longer within distance to hear her.

She picked herself up after a period of time, then looked around with a sudden feeling of confidence for a better life. This life they described burned in her heart. Now she would not give up.

She ran into her little house and dug out the coins she had saved, which she had stashed out of sight. She had hidden the coins carefully to keep the other slaves host. No one knew of the money but Befana.

She counted out the price that her master had quoted her to buy her freedom. She slipped the amount under the door of the main house. She put everything she had in a small cloth pouch. She readied herself for travel, placed her scarf on her head, and carrying her broom, she started her journey to find the child.

Befana started to wander the streets, at first calling the names, "Caspar, Melchior, Balthasar..." But after a while stopped calling as the only response rendered was from angry residents that she awoken.

Then it struck her, she would look into the windows of the homes at the children sleeping. She might be given a sign so she could recognize the holy child, the child destined to be king.

Every child she looked upon appeared to be so sweet in the state of sleep that she decided to leave a small gift for each. Each child had the possibility of being the Christ child and her lack of faith did not allow her to recognize it. One night turned into days, one night and another and another. She cashed in her savings and cleaned during the day for people so that she could buy the small gifts and provide for herself.

People seemed to need her service. At first, her appearance repelled them. But when she spoke so sincerely, they took her in to hear the story of the night with the strange men and the promise of love. Maybe, it was the experience with the Magi. Or it could have been her passion to find the freedom that she sought. Either way, she found a peace she had never known before.

La Befana continued to search for the Christ child for many years until her body failed and faded away. Her spirit lives forever in the peace conveyed upon her by the three wise men and her search of the ultimate love.

To this very day, La Befana searches. Once a year, she continues to visit every child in Italy. She leaves treats for each child while awaiting the finding of the special child of love and peace, the one and only Christ child.

Italian children in return know she will come on the Feast of the Three Kings, what she seeks, and await her visit.

Just as Befana and the Magi, the wise still seek Him.

Conclusion

For many, the Christmas season causes sadness as much as it brings joy. The same season which we celebrate can cause depression as we remember Christmas past. Hopefully, the Twelve Days of Christmas stories will help evoke only love, both agape and philos. Find the one aspect of hope in each situation and hang onto the good that it brought.

Just as parents rejoice in the birth of their new child, they also suffer anxiety of how to care for the child. The two opposites representing the universal balance of life. Jesus Christ was born in a time of Roman Empire dominance under the rule of Augustus Caesar, who thought he, himself, was a god. The Empire rule was enforced by a brutal military force which held their strength of conquest over the value of human life. Hundreds upon thousands of people were crucified. Sometimes crosses bearing those murdered lined an entrance to a city. Into this world came the words, "Love one another as I have loved you."

Truly, civilization needed God's love made human over 2000 years ago which provides hope that it is never too late for God's being in our world now.

The connection to the original Christmas and the generations of people who have celebrated the season for the last two thousand years comes through stories. We have struggled over the centuries, but we have kept our faith. Build a circle of love around you and your family through trust and understanding. Come to celebrate the light, through the birth of Jesus Christ.

*I wish you all a Merry and
Blessed Christmas . . .
Every day of the year.*

About C.C. Cargnoni

CHRISTINE BUILDS HER communication skills through membership in Toastmasters International. She believes that communication creates understanding and trust so fully that she became a Distinguished Toastmaster so she could deliver her message more effectively.

Storytelling has developed into a big part of creating understanding through shared experiences. It gives the reader or listener the opportunity to put themselves in the place of the storyteller.

Storytelling also serves to create a firm generational foundation for families. The experiences of grandparents reflect upon their children, and then upon their grandchildren. Storytelling builds bonds among family members.

Learn more about C.C. Cargnoni at:
ChristineCargnoni.com

Order multiple copies of *Love Among Us –
The Twelve Days of Christmas* by emailing:
Love12DaysofChristmas@gmail.com

CPSIA information can be obtained
at www.ICGtesting.com
Printed in the USA
BVHW061234231121
622339BV00009B/310